GW00381357

FRIEDRICH HARRIS

SHOOTING THE HERO

Other books by Philip Purser

Peregrination 22

Four Days to the Fireworks

The Twentymen

Night of Glass

The Holy Father's Navy

The Last Great Tram Race

Where Is He Now?

The One and Only Phyllis Dixey
(with Jenny Wilkes)

A Small Explosion

Halliwell's Television Companion
(with Leslie Halliwell)

FRIEDRICH HARRIS
SHOOTING THE HERO

Philip Purser

Quartet Books
London   New York

First published by Quartet Books Limited 1990
A member of the Namara Group
27/29 Goodge Street, London W1P 1FD

Copyright © by Philip Purser 1990

British Library Cataloguing in Publication Data
Purser, Philip
Friedrich Harris: shooting the hero.
I. Title
823.914 [F]

ISBN 0-7043-2759-7

Typeset by MC Typeset Ltd, Gillingham, Kent
Printed and bound in Great Britain by
BPCC Hazell Books
Aylesbury, Bucks, England
Member of BPCC Ltd

When I watched him in one or other of those stupid roles of his old age; when for example he played the Jewish poppa in a vile remake of *The Jazz Singer*, or on television a Roman elder in some laughable epic continuing over two or four evenings; when he was inveigled on to one of those ceremonies at which today's film makers 'salute' each other, and he would address them in the quavering voice he affected on such occasions; when I saw these things and remembered how once he could strike fire, summon music and bring down thunder with one cry, then I would groan aloud that I had not killed Laurence Olivier when I had the chance.

Now he is dead and all he did is to be treasured. Or almost all. From the store of video-cassettes which constitute the toy cinemathéque of my own declining years, I may see his Hamlet, his Richard, his pink-skulled Lear, his most interesting, powerful homosexual in the English television play *The Collection* of Harold Pinter. I have also *That Hamilton Woman*, as *Lady Hamilton* became in America, taken from an early a.m. transmission on Station

1

K-something-or-other, Arkansas, so interrupted by commercials, so subject to interference and so mutilated a print even before it got on the air that what remains is merely a puzzle. But of the Olivier movie above all Olivier movies I might have been expected to play and play again I have – or until last month had – no copy.

There came in the mail a padded bag stuck with many English stamps and a demand for $6.70 in customs dues and handling charges. Inside was a cassette, also a note from Martin Kilner. After all these years! From Martin! He said that *Henry V* had been put out by the BBC as a tribute to the great man, together with some pious remembrances. He thought I might like a copy he had recorded off air. I wondered what could have fired such a generous impulse.

He wrote that Robert Krasker and Esmond Knight had died previously, there weren't so many of us left. Also that some young English smart-arse was remaking the title. Jesus, is nothing sacred? I shall take care not to see it.

I turn the cassette over in my hands, marvelling or regretting that so much can these days be contained in so little. The only flaw is that European and American video standards are not the same. To play the cassette I must drive to the Film School, where I continue to take two classes a week, namely 'Film in the Third Reich' and 'The Hollywood Majors in Decline, 1951–1970'. In one of the seminar rooms are a VHS recorder and a Philips TV to the 625-line PAL system, as developed by a Dr Walter Bruch who, I used to tell my students until I tired of their lack of response, had previously worked on the V–1 secret weapon directed against England in 1944, unfortunately too late to do a lot of good. Lips moving as they wrote, they would transcribe this in their notebooks without frowning, without smiling, without betraying any process that had intervened between ear and hand.

I wait until everyone has gone, so that I shall not be interrupted. I close the curtains against the noise and the wheeling lights of the freeway (what other university would have a freeway straddling the campus?) and make myself comfortable with a can of Coors and a small Yankee cigar.

I had forgotton the brilliance of the colour that Krasker won from that one irreplaceable Technicolor camera, the spell of the words, the thrill of the music. The action builds towards the most famous charge in cinema history. The French knights are hoisted aboard their mounts, the English drive their pointed stakes into the ground, the braggart Dauphin drains his stirrup cup. Trumpets sound. Slowly, ploddingly the horsemen begin their advance. The plod becomes a trot, the trot a canter. Finally they break into a gallop, the black-armoured Constable of France drawing ever farther ahead. I find myself straining forward, searching into the picture only to seek beside the long green slope, the distant trees, the charging knights, some proof – a stray shadow, perhaps, or the canvas satchel that stupidly I left lying within camera sight until Krasker swore and I dashed headlong to seize it – that so many years ago, yes! I really was there, caught up in such unbelievable fashion in the creation of this

3

movie that still gleams like a prodigious jewel.

The bowmen strain their bows, the King on his white horse drops his sword in signal, and the music cuts to the unearthly sound of the arrows as they arch their way into the sky to rain down on the foe. But after only a few moments of the ensuing battle I still the picture with the remote control. My head aches from over-fierce concentration too close to the screen. The beer has left a sour taste in my mouth. The janitor, who has looked in once on his rounds, will soon be back. Most of all, I am not ready yet to face again the duel when the King meets the Constable of France in mortal combat.

There is something else I have shirked too long, another film I should see again. Alas, no cassette exists that I know of, nor has this picture ever been shown in the United States. Last year it was screened on French television, I am told, with the narrative interrupted for the interpolation of newsreel material about the Nazi régime. I did not see it. I have not been in Europe since 1975. I can only recall *Kolberg* from thirty years before that, watching it tired and hungry in a beleagured city, the pioneer corporal by my side snorting, 'Why did they not send sausage? Or schnapps? Anything instead of this!' Even so, as its vistas unfold again in my memory, its vast armies march, its horsemen also charge and its heroes declaim, I swear that it deserves better than to have sermons pasted upon it. For those who must have sermons, it is sermon enough in itself: a monument or, as Goebbels himself decreed, a 'colossal fresco' to an empire built on lurid and foul dreams.

One

But to begin at the beginning and to begin with Josef Goebbels, join me in the private cinema of the official residence of the Reichsminister for Popular Enlightenment and Propaganda at Hermann Göringstrasse 20, an address the Reichsminister increasingly resented. I cannot be precise as to the exact date in 1943. It would have been April already, I guess. I seem to remember the Easter sales in the big stores, buds bursting out on the trees, and the damned RAF raids on Berlin which broke many a night's sleep about this time.

Goebbels also had cinemas in the family villa on Schwanenwerden Island and in his lakeside place at Lanke. To watch a film was the relaxation at the end of the day that he preferred to any other, save entertaining a pretty young actress from the film studios. Sometimes, of course, the two pleasures could be combined, especially at Lanke. But since he had made his 'Total War' proclamation in February, calling on the people to apply themselves only to work and duty, pleasure had been rather out of fashion. Oh, the fight he had with Göring over

Horcher's, the restaurant in Lutherstrasse the Luftwaffe top brass frequented! Goebbels wanted to close it as ostentatious luxury, Göring countered by threatening to reopen it next day as an officers' club. They had screamed at each other by telephone for half an hour according to the Promi switchboard operator.

Even these end-of-the-day picture shows had to put duty first and relaxation second if there was a film awaiting ministerial inspection. When there were guests, the dinner beforehand was famously plain. Herrings and potatoes, everyone remembers in the memoirs of the period. I don't know if that had been the menu this night, for as Goebbels's filmadjudant (classy title, insignificant job) I was not invited. There would be stiff-suited representatives of various ministries, a newspaper editor or two, a war hero perhaps, and the remainder from the filmworld. Some wives and mistresses were expected to be brought, others not. As they filed into the theatre much agony went into deciding where to sit. Too close to Goebbels and you could risk his displeasure. Too far away, you put yourself on the outside of the magic circle.

This night one fellow had no qualms about cramming his bulk into one of the favoured seats reserved for the Reichsminister's special guests. Who else but Heinrich George, naturally? The great actor to be numbered with Emil Jannings and Werner Krauss as the dreadnoughts of the German theatre and cinema! Oh, he had a bluster about him. He could fill the screen well enough. But he was gross and grizzled and fifty years old, and his temper had given me some bad moments when I was at the studios. Besides, it was disgraceful that someone with such a past as his should be fêted and given fine rôles in loyal German films.

He must have dimly recognized my face from former days, and mouthed a greeting. I chose not to notice it, and looked away.

It was then that I saw the figure, hanging back at the rear of the small auditorium, who was to change the course of my destiny. What was his name? Of course – von Damitz. When I was seconded to the Ministry in 1941 he was Goebbels's personal adjudant. Already he wore the uniform of the Waffen–SS. Quite a few of Goebbels's staff contrived to wear SS uniform, for example von Damitz's successor Schwägermann, who now stood respectfully at his side, but not that of the combat branch, nor with a ribbon from the drive into France.

Now he had added the Knight's Cross to the Iron Cross and the dark red and black ribbon to the medal the troops called the 'Order of Frozen Meat' for service on the Eastfront. His rank badges were of a *Sturmbannführer* or major. Thinning hair made him look older than he was, which would have been about thirty. He held one arm stiffly to his side, a raw new scar dragged his mouth down at the corner.

He must have caught my stare and gave me a penetrating look before turning to Schwägermann and asking something. Schwägermann's lips shaped my name.

I hauled myself back to my duties.

'Is the Reichsminister ready?' I murmured to Goebbels.

7

'Yes, yes,' he said impatiently, as he always did. Everyone will know what *he* looked like – the lively-boy features, at this time rather drawn after a kidney-stone illness; the sun-tan winter and summer, by arrangement with an ultra-violet lamp; the clumsy foot, the bright eyes. It is not so easy to sketch in the charm, the power, the magnetism, the sarcasm or the venom that could fill him one instant and be gone the next. As the lights dimmed, he reached inside his jacket and unfolded his spectacles. He was vain about not being seen to wear them.

The film was an enemy propaganda effort, obtained through one of the embassies. It was supposed to be set in the Reichs-protectorate of the Netherlands.

'What does it mean idiomatically, the name of this film?' Goebbels demanded as the titles came up. He liked to give the impression that he knew English well, but of course it was legitimate to query a fine shade of meaning.

'*The Silver Flotilla*,' I said, giving him the absolutely literal translation, 'or perhaps *The Silver Fleet*. For the benefit of any of the Reichsminister's guests who do not understand English, it concerns a Netherlands shipbuilder who is building a new U-boat for the Reich . . .'

I could just see Goebbels slapping his hand up. 'Thank you,' he snapped. He turned to the most august of his guests. 'If a film cannot tell its story in pictures, it is no film, eh?'

'Up to a point, Herr Doktor,' said the guest comfortably. He was the director Veit Harlan, lately named by Goebbels as a Professor of the German Cinema. He was successful, trusted and popular. His latest, *The Golden City*, was a hit everywhere. He had begun as an actor and still had an actor's look about him, the thick hair brushed back from the temples, the handsome if by now rather heavy features, the expensive clothes casually worn. He could have been the middle-aged man of the world who charms the innocent young girl in one of those boulevard movies of the 1930s, except that he didn't need to charm innocent girls. He had one of his own by his side: his wife Kristina Soderbaum.

I squinted obliquely at her in the dimness of the theatre, waiting for a high-lit scene to reflect a little illumination. She was never glamorous in that lacquered-goddess Hollywood style that movie industries everywhere tried to emulate. She had a snub nose, a chubby face, a little-girl voice. Even when she had her hair up and long ear-drops, as this evening, she was a girl who could imaginably be living in the next block to you or working behind the perfume counter at Wertheim's. There was a scene in *The Golden City* in which, as the country girl in big sophisticated Prague, she is seduced by her worldly cousin. She played it fully dressed, not showing a square centimetre of flesh. It was still the most erotic thing I'd seen at twenty-three, because under the arms of her dress were dark sweat patches.

The Silver Fleet wound its way on. It was routine propaganda stuff but not without filmworld interest. The scenarist was the Hungarian Jew Pressburger who had worked at Ufa until it was time to take the

9

train. One of the actors I remembered also from Ufa days.

I let my gaze wander next to von Damitz. What was he doing here again? What was his interest in a minor figure such as Friedrich Harris? The 'Harris' was English, or Irish as I insisted, but there were plenty of higher-ups with more alien-sounding names. My antecedents had long ago been established. Nor could I have been seconded to the Ministry without the most thorough examination of my loyalty. So what else might be dangerous? I was still a civilian in a nation given over to jackboots and tunics, but so were many others in government service. It was no choice of mine. I had been turned down because of poor eyesight when I tried to volunteer in 1939; you did not often see Stuka pilots with glasses like beer-bottle bottoms. Thereafter my conscription had been deferred first at the request of the studios, subsequently on the application of the Ministry. As soon as a certain golden opportunity which hovered in the offing could be realized, then of course I would be off to carry a rifle or steer a tank.

Shit! Goebbels was glaring at me. 'His name,' he said. 'What is this actor's name?'

Obediently I peered at the summary paper, which in this light meant pushing up my glasses and holding it about ten centimetres from my eyes, never very impressive. 'Ralph Richardson,' I said. 'He is a Shakespearean specialist . . .'

'Not that one. Everyone knows Richardson. The other, who plays the so-called German officer and has strange eyes and a distorted face.'

I had no need to check this name. I knew him all right. 'Esmond Knight,' I said.

'*K*night,' said Goebbels, pronouncing the *K*. 'Of course. One should have remembered. He made something for Ufa here in Neubabelsberg. It must have been eight or nine years ago. Stop the film a moment.'

I signalled to the projectionist. Goebbels slipped his glasses back into his pocket as the lights came up. He said, 'It was called *Black Roses* if I remember correctly. We made versions in English and French as well as German. This Esmond Knight was in the English version.

'I saw it,' squeaked Kristina, clapping her hands. 'It made me cry.'

Goebbels gave her a smile but addressed himself to the rest of the guests. 'Interestingly,' he said, 'the theme of *Black Roses* was the resistance of Finnish patriots to the Russian imperialists who sought to seize their country in Tsarist times. Esmond Knight played the part of one of these heroes, clear-eyed and fresh-faced.'

It should have been clear to all by now that the Minister had been brushing up his subject. He excelled at seemingly impromptu little speeches to receptive audiences, such as the foreign journalists when they came to the Promi for a briefing. It made little difference whether he had five or fifty hearers. His face would light up, his hand pluck phrases from the air. He had a mellifluous speaking voice, and this level of address – pitched above conversation but well below the ranting and raving he turned on for the Sportpalast masses – suited it best. He would have been dangerously good on TV.

'Today,' he was saying, 'we could film the same story brought up to date. We could set it in the winter of 1939–40, when once again brave Finnish patriots were resisting the Russians and the English talked of sending a brigade of soldiers to help them. Just think – we might have ended up on the same side! But now the Russians are the honoured allies of the British, both are at war with Germany, and Mr Esmond Knight must have his face disfigured in order to perform as some kind of monster in German uniform.'

I had this foolhardy impulse to set the facts right. 'Excuse me, Herr Doktor, but apparently he had been wounded in a sea battle.'

Goebbels glared.

'That is to say, the disfigurement is not the work of the make-up artist. His ship was hit by a shell from the *Bismarck* and he has lost his sight.'

'I am glad to learn our warships contrived to hit *something*,' Goebbels said icily, at which there were some respectful sniggers from his audience, so I was probably forgiven my interruption. He gestured towards the blank screen. 'Does anyone wish to see more?'

No one did.

Goebbels sighed. 'You may be thinking I rejoice to see such clumsy propaganda from the enemy. On the contrary, I mourn to see such prostitution of the art of the cinema. Imagine the reactions of the audience in Lisbon or Paris or Stockholm' – with a little inclination of the head towards Kristina Soderbaum, because she was Swedish – 'when presented with such rubbish as we have just seen. They are perhaps quite held by the tensions of the story. But what will linger on in their minds? Something about a foolhardy Netherlander acting against the best interests of his country, which they know will prosper under our New Order. And a caricature of a German officer with a twisted face which they will instinctively reject as an English calumny.'

I might have saved my breath. To Goebbels, even an injury in battle was a conspiracy of the enemy.

'How infinitely subtle, cultured and effective are our own films by comparison,' he continued. 'Consider, for example, *Friedrich Schiller: Triumph of a Genius*. By his side, Heinrich George nodded his bristly head, for he had played in that film.

Imagine you are a Swiss or an Argentinian. What is this that emanates from a Fascist dictatorship, as you have probably been led to regard the Third Reich? A film whose hero rebels against authority and champions free speech! That hardly accords with the lies you have been told. Yet for us privileged to live in the Third Reich it is equally a hymn to a hero who can see beyond the limits of petty principalities to a vision of the great Germany which will one day arise – and in our day has arisen, gentlemen!'

What he didn't mention, though it must have given him quiet satisfaction, was that all Berlin had been smirking at Schiller's antagonist in the picture, the Duke of Württemberg. Heinrich George had played him as a porky autocrat whose great arse jutted out beneath his coat-tails, who fancied himself as a military commander and connoisseur of works of art! The likeness to Göring was irresistible.

Anyway, everyone clapped, if in Harlan's case without great enthusiasm. *Schiller* wasn't his.

'Then only a few weeks ago,' Goebbels went on, 'we have held the grand première of *Munchhausen*, the film to celebrate twenty-five years of Ufa. Soon that will be charming audiences everywhere with its wit and magic and the brilliant colours of our German Agfacolor process. But how, you will perhaps ask, does that bear on our historic struggle for the destiny of Europe? What is the propaganda value of a film about a man who rides on a cannon-ball, sets his watch by a living clock, voyages to the moon and talks to a human head growing as a flower on a stalk?' –

Or for that matter gazes on naked beauties bathing in an Ottoman harem, which was the scene in the film that had everyone talking.

'What will it mean to our soldiers on the Eastfront when they watch *Munchhausen* in the mobile kino?' He glanced at his old adjutant. 'Can you tell us, Sturmbannführer von Damitz?'

'They will like the harem bath scene.'

Goebbels smiled, which was the cue for everyone to risk a small laugh; everyone except Harlan again, that is. This wasn't his picture either.

'As for audiences in other countries,' Goebbels went on, 'I will tell you what they will be thinking as they stream away from two hours of enchantment. They will be thinking that for a country at war to be able to make such an extravaganza, it must be confident of victory.'

After another flutter of applause it was Harlan's

turn at last.

'Finally,' said Goebbels, 'Professor Harlan and Fräulein Soderbaum have just returned from a visit to Sweden to launch there *The Golden City*, another beautiful colour film, romantic yet realistic' –

The dark sweat patches, for instance –

'And carrying a clear message for all Aryan peoples that, without love for the soil of their native land, there can be no love at all.'

Sure it had, after Goebbels had personally insisted that the country cousin played by Kristina should atone for preferring city lights to her native soil. The screenplay had been rewritten so that she finished up back home drowning herself. Harlan had turned necessity into virtue with a marvellous scene in which a search party with flickering torches sought her along the shores of the marsh.

Goebbels was coming to Kristina. 'Frau Harlan has of course accompanied her husband on this visit to what is, after all, her native land. Perhaps she would tell us a little about it.'

'Oh, the film has been a great hit. Everyone talks of it. Veit has lectured twice, to the International Club and at Uppsala, to the university!' She took Harlan's arm, smiling prettily. 'We have been made honorary students, with the white cap, you know. And your ambassador – *our* ambassador, I should say – has given a great party for us at the Grand Hotel. It was the most fashionable night Stockholm had seen for ages.'

She directed the smile, diplomatically, at the man from the Foreign Ministry, Heims, who looked gratified. The Foreign Ministry was not always popular in Goebbels's circle, in fact rather rarely.

Suddenly von Damitz posed a question. 'May one ask if the professor or his gracious wife saw any indication of the enemy films enjoying a comparable success?'

Kristina half-opened her mouth as if to reply, glanced at Harlan, closed it again.

Harlan said, 'Nothing of note.'

'One hears of a film called *Pimpernel Smith* with the actor Howard, Leslie Howard.'

'More crude rubbish,' snapped Goebbels. 'An English professor who rescues Jews and criminals from detention in what is supposed to be Germany. Needless to say, we are again depicted as monsters and fiends.'

'But this film is banned in Sweden as war propaganda,' cried Heims. 'We have been repeatedly assured so by the Swedish authorities.'

'The English continue to project it over and over again in their embassy,' said von Damitz. 'To gain an invitation to one of these screenings has become almost as sought after as an invitation to meet Fräulein Soderbaum.' He gave her a little bow which only stiffened the irony of his voice. 'With respect, Herr Reichsminister, our information is that this film has been extremely effective in other neutral countries, notably Spain, Portugal and Ireland.'

'Ireland!' exclaimed Heims sarcastically.

'A non-belligerent not without importance both to the enemy and ourselves,' snapped von Damitz.

Harlan broke the silence that followed. 'Of course, the attraction is Mr Howard first, and Mr

Howard also second and third and fourth, with the film itself of minor interest. Since *Gone with the Wind* he is a great star all over the world.'

This was a cunning scent to lay, since it was well known that *Gone with the Wind* was another of Goebbels's favourite movies, screened in this very cinema several times. Nor did he ever conceal his admiration for it.

'That is very true,' he said. 'Whether one makes clumsy propaganda or artistic propaganda, the film actor or actress is ultimately the person who must convey it to the audience one wishes to influence. Which is why we are fortunate to have the services of such talented and attractive stars as Fräulein Soderbaum here.' He led the assembly in another little hand-clap. Kristina put on a demure look.

'Supposing I now let you into a secret,' Goebbels said suddenly, his voice rising. He let the expectant silence that followed hang in the air for a moment. 'The secret is that we are now planning the greatest film ever made, a film that will make *Gone with the Wind* seem like an insignificant trifle. A film that will set the seal on all that the German nation has already achieved and will soon complete. A film that in a thousand years will still be watched in wonder by the peoples of the world. Gentlemen – and Fräulein Soderbaum – you will be proud to tell your grandchildren that you were among the first to hear of it.'

My heart gave a cautious leap. Did he really mean it? Was the project on which so many confidential memoranda had circulated, so many proposals been put forward, finally going ahead? On such an outcome all my hopes of filmglory depended. Unless it happened soon, I had resolved to seek my laurels elsewhere.

Goebbels looked at his watch. 'But I am keeping you from affairs of state, gentlemen,' he said to the officials. 'Or should I say from some well-earned rest at the end of a day of affairs of state? I think the English will not be over tonight.' For the editors, he made some playful reference to deadlines.

As they obediently allowed themselves to be shepherded out, I busied myself with preparations for the remainder of the evening.

'Good evening, Harris.'

I hardly needed to turn my head to know it was von Damitz. I bowed and foolishly extended my hand, remembering too late the right arm that he kept to his side and which, I now saw, ended in a leather glove. Close to, his face had a softness, even a petulance, save for the jagged scar at the corner of the mouth.

'That was a most interesting résumé of our film propaganda,' he said softly. 'Except that no mention was made of another film Professor Harlan was to have made. It was being planned even in my time here: the film *Narvik*, about the brilliant campaign of the German forces in Norway three years ago.'

I knew of it, of course. The project had dragged on until quite recently. The navy was especially keen, having won some small glory there. Harlan had been up to Narvik only in January to see what forces were available to refight the landings. But finally the whole idea had been dropped. I explained as much.

'But do you know why it was abandoned?'

I had an inkling but did not like to voice it.

'I will tell you,' von Damitz said. 'It was because the English heard about it and sent a message that if the filming went ahead they would fly over and bomb it. That is propaganda of another kind, is is not?'

I nodded.

He said, 'I must catch up with all the news of the filmworld.'

'You seem very well informed as it is.'

'Not concerning the gossip of the studios and so on. It would be useful to have some talk with you.'

'At your service, Herr Sturmbannführer. You know where to find me.'

'I shall,' he said.

'Good,' said Goebbels when only the Harlans remained. 'Now we can enjoy a real film. But first some more brandy.' He signalled the flunkey who hovered unregarded at these occasions. However unappetizing the food, the liquor was always good. 'I am sorry to have inflicted that other rubbish upon you, but all the time the demand is being made – by other ministries, the High Command, party departments – that our films should be more like the insult we have just sampled. We should show the English flogging their native troops or Churchill drunkenly sending his airmen to drop bombs on hospitals and schools. I make out the case you have heard me make tonight, and six months later I must make it all over again.' He sighed, then indicated the seats on either side of his. 'Come and sit by me.'

Veit took the seat on the far side from where I stood, Kristina the nearer. Goebbels smiled and patted her hand.

'What are we going to see?' she asked. 'Is it *Gone with the Wind*?'

He shook his head. 'All three hours of it! I think I would have the Head of Studio complaining tomorrow of an exhausted film star.'

'*The Thief of Baghdad*?'

'Ah, you are getting closer.' He turned to Harlan. 'A little business with the pleasure for you, Herr Professor. I want you to tell me what you think of the leading actor.'

The lights dimmed. Goebbels slipped on his glasses. The titles began to fill the screen.

'I know what it is!' cried Kristina. I saw Harlan try to signal to her, too late. 'It is *Lady Hamilton*.'

'You have already seen it?' Goebbels showed his vexation. 'How? Where?'

'The film itself, no,' said Harlan quickly.

'But in Stockholm the film journals have been full of it,' said Kristina, recovering.

'Naturally,' said Goebbels sourly. But he patted her hand again.

The movie opens in Calais with a supposedly old and raddled Emma Hamilton confiding to a fellow derelict who and what she had been. The whole picture then on is a flash-back, a device I never liked a lot. For one thing, it was difficult to persuade vain actors and actresses to look sufficiently old and raddled in the framing sequences. The famous Vivien Leigh was no exception here. However, we were already being hauled back in time and place to the British residence in Napoli and the arrival there of the radiant young Emma and her Irish mother, as vulgar as any Kreuzberger tenement wife. I heard a tinkle of laughter and, even though it came from Kristina, was irritated. Why should this woman be mocked? Suddenly I was seeing the film as through Goebbels's eyes. Imagine how mother and daughter would immediately win the sympathy of all those who had suffered under the English ruling classes – the Americans, the Irish, the Indians. They would instinctively side with the women, expecting them to be insulted or patronized. But the very reverse was happening! This Emma, who had been little better than a strumpet, who had danced naked before men's eyes, was about to become the British ambassador's lady.

Oh, this was propaganda as cunning as anything Goebbels had extolled. And it was only a start. With Emma the audience would be led into the passionate love affair with the hero Nelson, and thus into the patriotic cause he personified. I peered at the summary paper to see who were the scenarists. Walter Reisch, another of our Jews who had fled to Hollywood or England. What would the enemy do without them? And R. C. Sherriff, whose name I remembered in connection with the anti-war play *Journey's End*. Evidently he had suspended his anti-war beliefs for the time being.

Harlan must have seen me looking at the paper. He signalled me to come closer and mouthed, 'Korda has directed this himself?'

I nodded.

'And the scenario?'

I whispered the names.

'Ssssh!' hissed Goebbels. 'And sit down.'

I sat down in the seat over which I was crouching, only two places from Kristina. She gave me a little smile. I could smell a fragrance coming off her, faint but alluring. All the French perfumes were still plentiful in the Berlin stores.

On screen, Nelson's ship was entering the harbour, thundering out a salute of gunfire. Emma darted from her bed on to the balcony to see what the commotion was about, her nightdress fluttering against the morning sunlight. It was clever, it was damned clever. She was seizing a spyglass. The picture shaped itself to the blurred, round image of the telescope, the wooden sides of the warship, the smoking guns each framed in its port. Then the camera tilted as Emma searched upwards; mast, sails, rigging, the English flag and a burst of martial music on the soundtrack. In a moment she would have her first glimpse, which would also be our first glimpse, of the fate in store for her.

A small boat was being rowed ashore. Between the broad backs of the sailors could be discerned a figure seated just in front of the helmsman. He wore a cocked hat and orders upon his breast. Cut to a closer shot. He sat straight but seemingly reposed, looking ahead expectantly. The suspicion of a smile lightened the keen features above the deeply cleft chin. It was the eyes, though, that seized attention – dark, intense, magnetic.

I felt a touch on my arm, as light as if a little bird had lit. I turned my head towards Kristina's.

'His eye,' she whispered. 'I thought Nelson had

22

only one eye.'

'Soon. In the next battle, I think.'

'Should I know him?' Veit Harlan was asking.

'Olivier,' said Goebbels, accenting the first syllable. 'Laurence Olivier.'

The film continued without further interruption until near the end when, in the moment of victory at the sea-battle of Trafalgar, Nelson was struck by a marksman's bullet. No sooner had he breathed his last than Goebbels spoke.

'Why have we no actors of such heroic magnetism?' His voice drowned the film sound, as if he had suddenly mounted the Sportpalast podium. 'Yes, yes, we have actors in their maturity with such a quality – Heinrich George, for example. We have some promising youngsters coming forward. But our actors who should be in their heroic prime, where are they? I will tell you. Because they had to learn their craft during the System-time, when our film industry was in the hands of Jews and pacifists and "heroism" was a notion for contempt, they simply do not exist. They were not bred! They learned only to play adulterers in decadent comedies.'

So the old fraud was still in favour. Well, he had prudently kept sober this evening. When he was in his cups he was not above mocking the regime which kept him in champagne and schnitzels. Everyone knew that in bad old Weimar days – the 'System-time' as the Nazis always termed it – he had been an out-and-out Communist. He had changed sides with a thoroughness remarkable even by the standards of 1933.

The story was coming to its conclusion, with Emma once more the old crone in the alley. Goebbels had taken off his spectacles and was clearly no longer interested. Harlan seemed also lost in thought. Only Kristina still gazed intently at the screen, her eyes glistening in the reflected light, her lips parted.

I slipped from my seat, ready to turn up the house lights and do whatever Goebbels should require next. This was probably the end of the evening, but you never knew.

As they rose from their seats Harlan said, 'Your Olivier is certainly a star. But if the Herr Doktor will forgive the question, what film does he have in mind that requires such a hero?'

This was a far from innocent question. Harlan was always juggling at least four possibilities for his next movie. The understanding seemed to be that for each epic he made to Goebbels's demands, he would be allowed one modest subject of his own choice. Since the collapse of the Narvik war film he had been busily canvassing the adaptation of a novel by Knut Hamsun, the Norwegian, and as Goebbels always professed great admiration for Hamsun, he must have been wondering if this was what the Reichsminister had in mind when he broke the news about the greatest film ever to be made.

He should have known by now that when Goebbels hoisted a flag it was seldom the flag you first supposed, and never the one you desired.

'Did I not make myself clear?' he said now. 'Forgive me, dear professor. I was thinking, of course, of the great film we shall make to the glory of the German people.'

As he held one of his favourite pauses I knew for certain – and with exultation – what he was going to say. He said, 'I have decided to reopen the possibility of making *Kolberg*.'

Poor Harlan was quite robbed of his worldly, actorly poise. He looked thunderstruck.

'I take it,' said Goebbels, 'that you would be gratified to take on that commission, if it were to be offered to you.'

Harlan managed a bow. 'Naturally,' he said in loud but noticeably flat tones.

'Good,' said Goebbels. 'And Harris!'

'Yes, Herr Reichsminister.'

'Let me have tomorrow a paper on all you can find out about this Olivier.'

SECRET

To: Reichsminister for Popular Enlightenment
            and Propaganda
From: Filmadjudant to the Reichsminister
Subject: The English actor Laurence Olivier

Reichsminister!

In futherance of your verbal instructions following
the informational screening of the enemy propaganda film *Lady Hamilton*, I have the honour to submit
the following report:

Olivier is thirty-five years of age. He is of Huguenot
blood, the son of a pastor in the English Church. I
can find no connection with our romantic painter
Friedrich Woldenar Olivier of Dessau (1791–1859).

As the Reichsminister will be aware, Olivier has
made one film for Ufa during the System-time, the
English-language version of *Hocus Pocus* (1930) with
Lilian Harvey. Curiously, the other English actor
the Reichsminister was discussing, Esmond Knight,
played against the same leading actress in his Ufa
film *Black Roses* of 1935.

At the time of the English fabrication of war in 1939
Olivier was in Hollywood. He has made *Wuthering
Heights* for the Jewish director William Wyler and
Rebecca with the Englishman Hitchcock. A further
reason for his presence in Hollywood was his attach-

ment to the actress Vivien Leigh who, of course, was making *Gone with the Wind* at this time.

Olivier and Leigh were married, each for the second time, shortly before they filmed *Lady Hamilton*.

They returned to England together in the first days of 1941.

Olivier had been taking private pilot lessons in America with a view to becoming a British naval flier. He now holds the rank of lieutenant but was evidently released from his duties to take part in the further propaganda film which will be known to the Reichsminister, *49th Parallel*. He has since been reported to be making a film called *Demi-Paradise*. Radio monitoring services report that Olivier has also participated in patriotic broadcasts.

Weighing these exertions against his delay in returning to England, one does not form the impression of a fanatical Churchillist. He might well be receptive to enlightened approaches. In the event of the warmongers Churchill and Roosevelt being replaced by wiser men, which the Reichsminister has more than once demonstrated to be a possibility, Olivier would certainly be a most valuable player in any film designed to popularize new world-political situations that might arise, for example England and America supporting our crusade against the Bolsheviks.

In particular the undersigned ventures to mention

the Reichsminister's plan for an epic film turning on the defence of Kolberg in 1806–7. Historically, English troops were landed to come to the aid of the town. Their commander could be played by Olivier. In the event of a less active stance being taken by the Anglo-Americans, i.e. a simple cessation of hostilities in the West, it would be even more important to enlist admiration for our German cause among the vast new 'neutral' audience that would ensue.

As the Reichsminister has acutely pointed out, German cinema has been deprived of actors in Olivier's age group who have the same heroic magnetism. With the Reichsminister's permission the undersigned will explore the *Kolberg* provisional scenario with a view to incorporating a role for such an actor should he become available.

Heil Hitler!

Harris
Filmadjudant to the Reichsminister

Two

The road between the Ufa studios in Neubabelsberg and the centre of Berlin includes a stretch of motor road whose two long straights, when joined at each end by steep banked curves, formed the Avus motor-racing circuit. I used to pretend to grumble with everyone else when two or three times a year the journey to work or the journey home again was disrupted to prepare for these carnivals of noise and fumes, but with young Martin Kilner I paid my way in one summer Sunday of 1937 to watch the Mercedes and Auto-Unions hurtling round. Some of them were fitted with futuristic enclosed bodies and attained speeds of nearly 300 kilometres per hour.

We never told the others. Goebbels was right. Even then, four and a half years after the coming to power of the Party, with most of the Jews long banished, Jewish worldliness and cynicism lingered on in the studios to corrupt the normal healthy interests of young German manhood. Neubabelsberg indeed! It was certainly still a new hill, if not a tower, of Babel when I first became a messenger boy. Englishmen, French, Italians, Swedish came and went. The first message I had ever to deliver to a sound stage was a telegram for Esmond Knight, on the set of *Black Roses*. As Goebbels had remarked, he was very different then from the squinting actor of the war film. He was dashing. He had bright eyes and fair hair. He wore a cravat at his neck and drove a little sports car. He ripped the telegram open and smiled and said, 'Jolly good!' When I asked him in English if there was any reply, he beamed again, said no there wasn't, thank you, and gave me the unheard-of tip of two Reichsmarks.

Today, in time of war, the Avus carried little traffic. We passed a military convoy, some lorries chugging along on producer gas, one tractor drawing a trailer. Official cars overtook us but hardly a private car at all. It looked as if Goebbels's exhortations to Total War were having an effect at last. There were orders both at the Ministry and the studios to use the S–Bahn whenever possible. Only the tins of film in the back of our small Opel and the pouch of official correspondence between my seat and that of Heinz, the stolid Promi driver, made our journey legitimate.

I had spent a successful morning. With the help of old Witters, the librarian, I had been able to unearth several interesting side-lights on Napoleonic history. I had also been able to show myself around the studios in a creative rather than a bureaucratic capacity. I had mingled with such former colleagues in the scenario department as remained. None had seemed unduly alarmed or surprised to see me – always a reassuring sign.

'What's the matter?' I said to Heinz. 'Why are

you stopping?'

He had no need to reply. A military staff car was crowding our little van into the side of the road, quite deliberately. I tugged on the window on my side to expostulate, but Heinz grunted to me to keep quiet.

A sergeant stepped from the car and saluted. He was wearing the uniform of the Waffen–SS.

'Herr Harris?'

'Yes.'

'Unfortunately, we have just missed you at the film studios and had to make pursuit. I apologize. Sturmbannführer von Damitz presents his compliments and would be grateful if you could see him on a matter of some urgency. I am to take you.'

I looked at Heinz. He grunted something to the effect that he would see the cans of film and message pouch were properly received. I got into the staff car. To my surprise we drove first to an area south of the Köpenickerstrasse which I knew well; my small apartment was just off the Michael-Kirchplatz, above a florist's shop. The car stopped outside it!

'The Sturmbannführer thought you might like to collect a toothbrush and pyjamas as we shall be going some way out of the city,' said the sergeant.

I gathered toilet articles, a clean shirt, spare socks and my cheque book. I stood for a moment, trying to see or think of anything that might be detrimental should I not return and the place be visited. My film magazines from America and England? To read them was only my duty. I told myself I was being melodramatic.

The car made for Friedrichstrasse and then

headed north, past the Tiergarten and out of the city by Glienicke and Birkenwerder. As signs for Oranienburg began to appear I had some moments of sickness for no one in Berlin could by now be unaware of the KZ (concentration camp) near this town. I told myself, as persuasively as I could, that the Waffen–SS had no part to play with the camps: their concerns were only military. Presently the driver took a side-road into forest land. I looked surreptiously to right and left but could see no watch towers. Now military signs appeared, saying simply 'Friedenthal'.

Presently we turned into the gates of an enclosed park and stopped by the guard-house. After frowning through the car window at me, the sentry raised the barrier and we drove on. Among the trees I saw several army huts, vehicles and a single tall slender tower whose purpose I could guess. At the end of the drive there stood an elegant small house of the Frederickan period; a hunting lodge as I learned later.

Conscious of curious eyes on me, I was led upstairs and along a corridor to a pine-panelled room furnished with a desk, filing cabinets, a military telephone, etcetera.

'Wait here,' said the sergeant.

Almost at once another door opened and von Damitz entered; behind him came an orderly carrying a tray.

'I thought you might like a cup of tea,' said von Damitz.

'Thank you.'

'The English are famous for their fondness for

tea, is that not so?'

I took the cup he proffered with his left hand. 'You would have been informed of all my circumstances when I was appointed filmadjudant to the reichsminister,' I said.

'Remind me.'

'My father was an English soldier or rather, an Irish soldier, with the so-called Army of the Rhine in Solingen after the betrayal of November 1918. My mother had lost her fiancé in the offensive of August of that year; he was an under-officer in the Westphalian Regiment. I was born in 1920, after my father had returned to Great Britain.'

He continued to regard me impassively.

'I neither praise her nor condemn her. She died when I was seven.'

'When you went to Ireland.'

'To England also. My father was constantly on the move in his efforts to remain ahead of the enemies and traitors who pursued him. My schoolroom was most often a third-class railway compartment, and the newspapers my reading book – '

'Ah yes, Walter Frederick Harris, the Irish patriot fighting the colonial occupier. Have I remembered correctly?'

I hesitated. 'That is what I have always wished to believe. He was a great one for talking. I shall always honour him for making himself responsible for me after my mother's death. But it may have been that there were additional reasons for our journeys, such as debts, etcetera.'

Von Damitz picked up a folder and flicked it open. 'Good. Our Irish department has no records of a republican campaigner of that name.'

'He died in an English prison. My hatred for England is no less.'

'You had already returned to Germany?'

'Exactly ten years ago. In the first months of the New Order. Even at twelve years of age I was swept up in the excitement, the intense patriotism all true Germans felt. My uncle took me to watch the torchlight parades. He had known hard times, he had been forced to move to Berlin from his beloved Rhineland in order to find work. Now things would be better, he told me.'

'He is a carpenter at the film studios?'

'The head carpenter. And it was he, naturally, who found for me a start there as a messenger boy.'

He glanced inside the folder again. 'From which you progressed by lucky chance to being an assistant on those hymns of ours to the Irish, *The Fox of Glenarvon* and *My Life for Ireland*, and thus to a place in the scenario department. You certainly have a gift of seeming to possess the right qualifications at the right time.'

For perhaps a whole minute he did not speak again but stared at me thoughtfully. At last he said, 'Of course, our propaganda effort is of paramount importance. But the other evening, as we discussed this film or that film actor, did you not feel that something was lacking?'

'I am not sure what the Sturmbannführer means.'

'Did it not all seem rather . . . bloodless? We talked, for example, of this so-called Englishman Leslie Howard who is apparently such a thorn in the flesh – that is the English idiom, is it not?'

35

I nodded. 'But why "so-called"?'

'He is, of course, a Hungarian Jew.'

I had not known that.

'Everyone agreed that his participation in the films *Pimpernel Smith*, etcetera, has done the English cause much good, and therefore our cause the same degree of harm. No one proposed any measures to correct this situation.'

He got up and, walking to the window, looked out into the park. He kept the hand with the leather glove stiffly to his side.

'Here we are setting up a military organization which will take direct action against the enemy in many fields of activity. I am to command a section whose targets will include their propagandists. To take Mr Leslie Howard again, how might we keep him out of mischief for a while, Harris? Or better still, for ever?'

'I'm not sure, Herr Sturmbannführer.'

'While he is safely in England, it would perhaps be difficult to ensure success. But suppose we were to learn that Mr Howard was expected shortly in neutral Portugal, to make propagandist appearances on behalf of his films and his country. That would make the game a little more evenly matched, would it not?'

Without expecting a reply, he strode back to his seat behind the table, opened the file again and took out a sheet of paper that looked familiar.

'On the other actor, Laurence Olivier, this is quite a good report of yours.' He looked up. 'You are surprised that I should have a copy? I must tell you that we belong to a sub-division of the State

Security Department.'

He perused the paper for a moment. 'You give the facts about this Olivier with commendable brevity as far as you know them. Unfortunately, your information stops considerably short of being up to date. You are not aware that he is about to make a patriotic film based on the play *Henry V* by William Shakespeare?'

'I have seen nothing of this in the foreign or enemy press.'

'We must see if we can keep you better informed.' He studied my report again. 'Tell me about the *Kolberg* film that we seem to be planning.'

'The inspiration is the heroic resistance to Napoleon's armies of the citizens of Kolberg, the fortress town of the Baltic – '

'I know where Kolberg is, thank you. My family takes its name from an estate not thirty kilometres away. But what happened to Kolberg? Tell me that!'

'After a bitter struggle it was taken by the French – '

'Exactly. So who is the inspiration – this matter of history – intended to impress? Is it to strengthen the morale of the German people by reminding them of a time when their native soil has been invaded, their armies defeated, their cities sacked? Is it to reassure our enemies that Germany is not invincible after all? Is it to reinforce the doubts of our unreliable allies and give occasion for thought to our fair-weather friends?' He added, 'If I recall my Shakespeare classes at Leipzig correctly, the English are at least taking good care to film a battle they won.'

I did not make a conscious decision to reply in

spirit. The impulse rose as if under its own power. 'The citizens of Kolberg were *not* defeated,' I cried, 'not in any true sense of the word. That would be the whole message of the film. When the commander of the garrison wished to surrender to the French without a shot being fired, they formed their own citizen militia and took over the defence of their town themselves. Armed only with pitchforks in some cases, they held up the French advance until they were overwhelmed. The story has long attracted the Reichsminister for its confirmation of the indomitable qualities of the ordinary German people.'

'As opposed,' said von Damitz, 'to the pusillanimity of the officer class?'

'There would be a more stalwart officer in the person of von Gneisenau.'

'Who has given his name to a warship which spends most of its time skulking in port.' He pondered for a moment. 'You say the Reichsminister has entertained this idea for some time?'

'From 1941, certainly.'

'When our armies were only advancing?'

'Yes. At that time the Reichsminister wished simply to make a German film on the scale of *Gone with the Wind*.'

'And now?'

This was dangerous again. I hesitated before replying: 'Should the war go worse for us before victory is finally won, the Reichsminister believes that such a film would indeed be the inspiration the nation would demand.'

'You mean if Bolshevik or Anglo-American forces

threaten our homeland?'

I could only signify assent.

He frowned. 'How long would this film take to produce?'

'On the epic scale envisaged by the Reichsminister, at least one year from authorization. At present, there is not even a screenplay – I have been hoping to be invited to work on it.'

'So we are talking about next year, possibly the end of next year?'

'Yes.'

The transformation was remarkable.

'That is different,' he said. 'That is only prudent.' He opened the folder again. 'Now about this wild idea of yours to involve the actor Olivier – our main advantage would be political, you say, were the English and the Americans to stand aside and allow us to pursue our crusade against Bolshevism?'

'Or even join us in it. The Reichsminister is a firm believer in such a possibility. In either case, it would be important to stress the heroic qualities of the German people while encouraging other nations to feel that they share our great European vision. The distribution of heroes and villains must be carefully balanced.'

'The citizens of Kolberg are the heroes. The French are the villains. What is the difficulty?'

'Unfortunately the Führer himself has decreed that Napoleon must be depicted only with respect. He has a great admiration for Napoleon.'

'I see.'

'Of course, one may show other Frenchmen in a less respectful light – as the Sturmbannführer will know, the essence of drama is the conflict between those who are on the same side but do not share the same nobility of character. We already have this on the German side. I have today been pursuing researches which promise an equally dramatic conflict on the French side.'

I paused.

'Go on,' he said.

'There were two of Napoleon's marshals leading the advance along the Baltic. We may assume they were rivals. One is determined to storm Kolberg at all costs and award himself the title Duke of Kolberg. The other sees no glory in senseless bloodshed and argues that the town may be persuaded to surrender.'

'And which marshal would Olivier portray?'

'One of them, Mortier, was half-English.'

'Ah! But is he the bloodthirsty soldier or the high-minded one?'

'That we would have to decide.'

Von Damitz unexpectedly smiled. The smile vanished as quickly as it had arrived. 'We come back,' he said, 'to the unreality of all these fine fancies of the Propaganda Ministry. How do you propose to lure Mr Olivier to Germany? Even if he agreed to come, which is scarcely possible, by which route would he travel?'

'The Sturmbannführer has perhaps fogotten that we are postulating a change in the world situation –'

'There you are again! If we wait for that to happen first, the film will be too late to help it happen.'

He took a key from his pocket and opened a drawer in the desk. I saw a folder marked with

'Highly Secret' warnings. He took out a slip of paper.

'You will tell no one what I am about to tell you. From our agents in Ireland we have learned that a party of English film-makers led by your heroic Olivier has just spent some days in Dublin in order to search out a suitable site where they may stage the battle sequences for *Henry V*. Apparently there are no unploughed fields in England and few horses – perhaps they have eaten them all. As I do not need to remind you, Harris, the southern part of Ireland is a neutral state with whom we maintain limited communications. What if we sent someone to negotiate with Olivier?'

'An interesting idea.'

He stood up. 'You have brought some overnight effects?'

'Yes, Herr Sturmbannführer.'

'Good. You start your training tomorrow. It will necessarily be rather condensed. There is not much time.'

We were accommodated in army huts, but with more space and comfort than that allotted to regular troops. My fellow students included a number of pioneers skilled in the use of explosives and quite a few *Marinesoldaten*. They seemed good fellows. There was a separate contingent of Waffen–SS who kept themselves to themselves. Von Damitz was much in evidence, of course, also a dark, powerful-looking brother officer called Skorzeny, later to win fame and high rank.

The foundation of our training was horse-riding,

though as things turned out for me not enough of the right kind. The instructors came from the Ritter–SS, a minor arm of the SS organization which attempted to combine the feudal order of the old landed estates with ideological nonsense about total mastery of man over beast. They were grooms and huntsmen and such fellows, given under-officer rank and by nature alternately subservient and bullying.

On one day only I was detached from the rest of my squad and told to report to von Damitz. He had with him an aged gentleman whose dress still included frock-coat and wing collar, together with spats over his shoes and, against any chill in the air, a rusty green mantle. No one could have been more out of place at Friedenthal.

'This is Professor Ludwig,' said von Damen. 'From my former university. He is an expert upon Panzer lore.'

I must have looked even more bemused.

'No, he is not going to teach you to drive a tank. I refer to the armour and weapons of medieval warriors, such as shall fight the battle of Agincourt over again.' In the presence of his old professor, he was in almost jovial mood.

For two hours I sat in a lecture hall while the professor droned on about grieves and cuirasses and chain mail. I stripped off my tunic and tried on some items, all too small for me. With my glasses removed, I forced a helmet over my head and waggled the vizor up and down and eventually managed to don my glasses again through the opening so that the professor swam into focus once more. He was peering at me rather perplexedly.

'You must wear those?'

'I'm afraid so, Herr Professor.'

'They were not customary.'

Afterwards we went to the riding-ring where, under the scowl of one of the instructors as well as the gaze of the professor, I saddled my usual nag with an elaborate structure into which I swung myself at the third attempt. Despite its raised back-rest and pommel I did not feel any more secure than usual, and a good deal less comfortable.

'Grip with your knees!' the instructor screamed monotonously, blind to the fact that my knees were now prised wide of the horse.

First a lance, then a sword, a shield and an axe were thrust into my gauntleted hand while the professor discoursed on their use and the instructor barked orders that were uniformly contrary to all the old gentleman was saying. Not content with this, the instructor disappeared while I was allowed to smoke my pipe for ten minutes, only to return mounted himself, and wearing a padded garment of the kind used for fencing. I was then subjected to various joustings each more humiliating than the last. He sent my sword spinning with his, smashed my shield with his axe – in vain the professor wailed that it was from the Stadtmuseum – and unseated me with his lance again and again until I was bruised all over.

It was when I was armed with the mace, or spiked hammer, against the instructor flourishing the axe again, that I spied von Damitz through a chink in my enclosing helmet. He stood by the side of the professor, handsome and smiling in the spring-time sunshine. I was suddenly determined not to be made a laughing-stock again. Anger gave me a rush of strength. My heels jabbed my horse's ribs so that he reared just as the instructor swung with his axe. The force of his exertion slowed him in his saddle. For an instant his bullet head and pock-marked neck seemed to float before me. I had instinctively raised the mace on high. I could bring it crashing down –

'Harris!'

As I hesitated, my horse returned to earth. The instructor's piggy eyes were on a level with mine, glaring.

'Gentlemen,' came von Damitz's voice again. 'That will do! Reserve your aggression for the enemy.'

Just as well: the handle of the mace sat easily in the grip. Its head weighed at least two kilogrammes. It was all too tempting.

We were instructed in the art of undergoing inter-rogation should we be captured, and how not be be caught out. For each man came a mock interroga-tion, rumoured to be an arduous experience. When my turn came I found myself facing von Damitz and a bleak civilian with the look of a policeman about him and a blue chin. I had no trouble defending my parentage and my failure to have become a soldier; von Damitz seemed to be shielding me from any-thing the other might say.

Abruptly, his mood changed. He said, 'We come now to your connection with the Kilner family.'

'The Kilner family?' I echoed as if striving to recall the name.

'Don't waste our time boxing. You know all too well what I mean.'

'Martin Kilner started at the Ufastadt as a young messenger boy when I was chief messenger. I had to knock some discipline into him as I had to do with all of them.'

'Did you take the others to swim at the Wannsee on summer Sundays, or drink beer and sing songs at Haus Vaterland? Were you invited to their homes as you were invited to the fine Kilner apartment on the Pariserstrasse?'

'It was not apparent that Martin Kilner was of Jewish blood. None of us guessed – '

'None of you thought it odd that the son of a prominent newspaper critic should be taken from school at the age of fifteen and arrive at the studios as a common messenger boy?'

'He said it was the best way to get into films.'

'With his father's connections, hardly necessary. Incidentally, what of the gossip there would have been around the studios concerning the race secrets of the Kilners, father and son?'

'In the filmworld such matters were late in coming to the forefront,' I muttered.

The other man spoke.

'When this *Mischling* was only fifteen you were already eighteen?'

'Only for a short while. Then he became sixteen.'

'It was still quite a difference in ages. A young man does not normally cultivate the friendship of a boy – but perhaps it was not normal, you and this Martin Kilner.'

I flushed a fierce shade of red and opened my

mouth to protest; he was already passing me a photograph. I had my arm around Martin's bare shoulder. Neither of us wore more than a bathing slip.

'It was a joke,' I said. 'While we waited for the delayed-action shutter release. It seemed it would never cease its buzzing.'

'And you still say you could see nothing Jewish about him?'

'Why should I? We were so alike we were sometimes taken for brothers.'

'But when he took his slip off, you would have seen something different then, eh?'

I flushed again.

'All right.' He passed me another photo.

It was of the small sister Luise in the dress she wore for her fourteenth birthday party. I remembered Martin taking the picture. At sixteen he already had a Zeiss Ikonta and dreamed of becoming a photo-journalist –

'What about this one?' the man was demanding.

'She was only a child.'

'She has breasts.'

I was not to be drawn on that.

'She is also of unmistakably Semitic features,' he bored on. 'When you were a guest in the Kilner household, Harris, you could not have failed to notice that, still less the flamboyant Jewishness of Frau Lottie Kilner, with her high colour and her furs and her heavy perfume?'

'At first I was deceived, I must admit. They were quite unlike the Jews I remembered from my childhood in Wedding, when many of them still wore a distinctive dress – '

'Try again,' said von Damitz.

'Later, of course, my eyes were opened, but it was common knowledge by then. Kilner was pulling every string to try and secure a post as a foreign correspondent. If they stayed in the Reich he would be required to divorce Frau Kilner on racial grounds.'

'Meanwhile the children were both sent to England?' said von Damitz.

'Yes. They went on the Kindertransport, to be taken into the home of some English family. Or so one heard.'

'Or so one heard? You would have learned directly and in detail of all that happened to Martin and the little Luise. Because you continued to call at the apartment on the Pariserstrasse.'

'Once or twice only! They had been kind to me, and they missed their children very much . . . '

The two pairs of eyes were cold.

'And to be frank, I hoped that Julius Kilner might help me in my ambition to become a film writer.'

'That is better,' said von Damitz. 'And did he?'

'I have heard nothing of him for two years.'

'For your information, he chose not to rid himself of the Jewess, and cannot therefore be employed by any newspaper, even if the profession of criticism were still allowed. He continues to earn a small income as a reader for the film company Tobis.'

When I made no immediate reply he added, 'You are not curious as to the fate of Frau Kilner?'

I shrugged.

'Supposing I told you she had been arrested and

sent to a concentration camp?'

'I would say it was the best place for her . . .'

The stiff arm swung with astonishing speed. The gloved fist boxed my ear with a force that nearly toppled me from my chair and left my head ringing.

'You do not give the reaction you think is wanted,' von Damitz said. 'You give the reaction that comes closest to your own disposition consistent with the identity you are assuming.'

'Very good, Herr Sturmbannführer.'

Towards the end of the course we were introduced formally to the parachute tower I had noticed when arriving at Friedenthal. My first jump was also my last as I badly wrenched my ankle on landing. Summoned to see von Damitz, I expected a reprimand, but he ignored my painful entry on a stick. He passed me a photograph. It showed a familiar-seeming figure in a light suit and sun glasses descending from an air-liner.

I studied it for a moment. 'Of course! The actor Leslie Howard.'

'On arrival in Lisbon' – he turned the print over to see the date stamped on the back – 'on the twenty-eighth. He will be returning in about four weeks. About the same time your admired Olivier will be starting his battle in Ireland.'

I waited.

'Are we all mad?' he demanded theatrically. And indeed there was a strange glint in his eyes.

'I am not sure that I follow the Sturmbannführer's meaning.'

'I mean that yesterday the English entered Tunis,

48

the Americans and so-called Free French took Bizerta, and on the Eastfront our armies were under heavy attack in the Kuban and Novorossiisk sectors. The Krupp works at Essen have been bombed for the fifty-fifth time. Dortmund has also been raided. And yet we make plans about films and film stars!'

I waited again.

He said, 'The propaganda is more important than the reality, eh?'

'On the other hand, Herr Sturmbannführer, it does seem that we have scored a true victory in that capacity with the Katyn revelations' – Goebbels had skilfully handled the discovery of the bodies of thousands of Polish officers and intellectuals buried in a forest near Smolensk. He had summoned an international commission to testify that they had been shot by the Russians in 1940.

'Perhaps, perhaps,' said von Damitz. 'Certainly that affair has put a strain on relations between the Bolsheviks and their allies.' He added drily, 'The Reichsminister is more convinced than ever that the Anglo-Americans will come over to our outlook. So your little operation shall go ahead. In fact your departure has been brought forward.'

I tried not to betray the mixture of fear and excitement which this calm announcement induced in me.

'Your foremost objective is to persuade Mr Olivier to come to us voluntarily. Failing that, you will bring him against his will. Failing this, you will endeavour to prevent his film of *Henry V* from being completed, by any means open to you. In the last resort you will at least deny his further services to

Churchill and the warmongers.'

'I am not sure I understand,' I said.

'By the same means,' said von Damitz patiently, 'that we plan to deny them the services of Mr Howard.'

Three

I will not dwell on the many interesting and some uncomfortable features of my journey to Ireland. Von Damitz would have preferred to devise some scheme whereby I could have been 'repatriated' under Red Cross auspices, for example, but there was simply no time. Normal diplomatic entry was ruled out because of the surveillance the Irish maintained over our embassy personnel; nor was the embassy 100 per cent dependable in the estimation of von Damitz's colleagues in the State Security Department. I travelled across Germany and France to the Atlantic port of La Rochelle, little knowing that I was destined to revisit that place in very different circumstances, and embarked aboard the U-608.

On the day of my departure from Berlin I was accorded the compliment of a brief meeting with Goebbels. The car bearing me into the capital made a detour to his country place at Lanke, where he was spending a rare day away from the office. Needless to say, it was not a day off. He was amply provided with dispatches, telegrams and other papers requiring his attention, and as soon as they were out of the way, he told me, his next article for *Das Reich* had to be composed. But, sitting in the sun in the garden, he looked incomparably better in health and spirits than when I had last seen him in the viewing theatre that night. He was wearing a cream-coloured suit which set off his tanned complexion to advantage.

He wished me success in my mission, though he seemed to have confused it in part with another of von Damitz's projects and said how important it was that the enemy's popular actors such as Leslie Howard should be prevented from spreading propaganda everywhere. We talked more generally of the cinema and he told me that once the war was won he was going to settle down to his long-held plan to write a work of film aesthetic to stand alongside Lessing's *Dramaturgie*. More immediately, alas, he was obliged once more to defend his aesthetic of the propaganda film against ignorant criticism. He extracted a letter from a number of letters he had set aside and scanned it angrily. It was from Reichsleiter Rosenberg, the so-called 'Philosopher of the Party' and these days Minister for the Occupied Territories of the East. After a moment Goebbels seemed to throw off his irritation and tossed the letter aside with a smile and the remark that it was not worth bothering about.

I ventured to raise the matter of *Kolberg* and my particular proposal about the 'good' and 'bad' French marshals. To my joy, he remembered them clearly and was most flattering and enthusiastic about my ideas. As soon as I returned from my special duties he would commission me to write the screenplay. Filled with excitement and resolve, I began to explain my scenario in finer detail but saw him consult his watch twice and steal a glance towards the lake, so rose to my feet with renewed assurances of loyalty and devotion. As I left, I recognized a pretty young actress from the studios making her way through the trees in a flowered summer dress.

The U-boat made rendezvous with an Irish fishing boat off the south coast of Ireland, and thirty-six hours later I slunk, or perhaps I should say 'stunk', ashore in a small fishing port. I had spent the last part of the voyage in the hold with the catch. Before that I had been very sea-sick. Before that there had been the confines of the submarine, reeking of diesel oil, battery fumes and the lavatory. I would have given one of the gold sovereigns I carried for a hot bath and change of clothing, but the fishermen seemed anxious that I should be gone from the vicinity as soon as possible. In the little I had seen of them before we berthed they had not shown much friendliness.

One of them now took me a short way until he could point out the railway station, then turned and was gone without another word. They had made me wait in the fish-hold until it was almost midnight and there was no sign of life around the station, which was lit by a single dim lamp. I wrapped myself in the English trenchcoat with which I had been provided, ate my last chocolate bar, carefully disposing of the wrapping, and stretched myself out on a hard seat on the platform.

I awoke, chilled and hungry, to early light. A

porter was sweeping the platform. 'Would it be the 5.45 you were planning to take?' he asked in an accent I found hard to understand. I must have muttered negatively or shaken my head while trying to grasp his meaning because he continued to the effect that this was just as well, as the 5.45 had not operated since soon after the Emergency began. If it was the seven o'clock I had in mind, that was not running either, but there was a departure every Tuesday and Friday in time to connect at Cork. I did not dare ask him if this day was a Friday or a Tuesday, nor even the name of the place, this being painted on the board only in the Gaelic form. Hunger and thirst did persuade me to ask where I might obtain a drink of tea and perhaps a piece of bread.

'A drink of tea?' he echoed, scratching his head. 'That is not easy with the tea being rationed to an ounce and a half. The bread is something else.' He returned a few minutes later with a bowl of milk and a wedge of soft bread with butter whose richness I can still taste after nearly half a century.

I must have dozed off again as the day warmed. I was woken next by the throbbing sound of an antiquated green motor bus that had drawn up outside the station. I was idly watching people board it when my benefactor reappeared.

'Is it that you're not going now?' he called.

'I wait for the train,' I said pleasantly.

'Ah, you see, the bus is the train.'

At this moment it began to move away with much smoke and noise. The porter uttered a piercing whistle and it stopped again. I had already gathered up my case and hurried out.

The bus was full of peasants, some of them nursing baskets of eggs or butter. As I squeezed my way to one of the remaining seats, there were many curious glances and a fellow smoking a clay pipe cleared his throat noisily and said something to the effect that I had certainly been in the company of fish. He did not seem to mean it pointedly, however, and as I became aware of many other smells – of tobacco, for example, and unwashed persons – my embarrassment faded. Purchasing a ticket from the conductor with the smallest note I had, of ten shillings, caused some confusion. Thereafter the journey proceeded uneventfully. In the city of Cork I boarded a train for Dublin, feeling quite safe among these simple people.

In Dublin I found my way to the small hotel or lodging house whose address in Hanover Street I had memorized, and after some attempts succeeded in making the prescribed telephone call. Though my father had spent much time in telephone call boxes as we travelled round England and Ireland, I had never faced the intricacies of Button 'A' and Button 'B' myself. It was something which might profitably have been taught at Friedenthal instead of, for example, the parachute. But the next day at noon I stood on a small bridge in the Zoological Gardens with a copy of the *Irish Times* in my hand. After some minutes a man of rather anxious appearance approached and leaned on the parapet of the bridge.

'A fine day,' I said in my best Irish manner.

'You would not have seen my dog?' he asked, with a slight German accent.

'What species of a dog?'

'Bulldog.'

We identified ourselves formally, though I was already satisfied that he was Carl-Heinz Petersen, who had been the German News Agency correspondent in Dublin until the outbreak of war, when he was invited to join our embassy as press attaché.

He said, 'I am not sure I understand the aim of this adventure.'

'Perhaps you should not try,' I snapped. 'It will be enough if you do what you are asked.'

'You are a brash young man. Perhaps they have not told you that every agent sent by the *Abwehr* has been caught by the Irish secret service or the police. They are not altogether the peasants of our sentimental belief.'

'You do not need to tell me that. I happen to be part-Irish myself. Nor am I from the incompetent *Abwehr*. I am sent by the *Reichssicherheitshauptamt*' – snapping out the title of this new organization in proud German.

He looked round nervously. 'Please be careful,' he whispered. 'Anyone might hear you. All right, you shall be put in contact with parties sympathetic to our cause.'

'The IRA?'

He made an expression of distaste. 'If you insist. They are narrow-minded, proletarian and unlikely to know the right people.'

'What is the alternative?'

'A more . . . romantic movement, with ideals closer to our own.'

'The Blueshirts?'

He nodded. 'Which do you prefer?'

It was absurd that I should be required to make the decision which might determine the success or otherwise of the mission. I said, 'Very well. The latter.'

'Good. Listen carefully. Write nothing down.'

When he had finished I thanked him, for he had been brisk and to the point. 'But why a bulldog?' I added. 'Why not a dachshound?'

'In the password, you mean?'

'Of course.'

He smiled ruefully. 'It derives from a silly joke maintained by my opposite number at the English legation. Apparently the English have a series of cheap adventure stories in which the villain happens to share my name, Carl Petersen, and the hero is called Bulldog Drummond. So this clown refers to himself as Bulldog Drummond and me as the villain Carl. In retaliation I let it be known that I have this stupid bulldog, Drummond, who follows me around and so often is lost.'

I liked him more for that.

I was to find my way to Dunleary, or Dun Laoghaire in the new-found Irish language fittingly called 'Erse'. It had struck me as a stupid choice, for this was the harbour used by the steamers plying between the Free State and England and therefore likely to be under regular scrutiny, but as I descended from the bus I realized that on the contrary the town was rather suitable. At least a dozen other people alighted here to go about some business or another. There was no danger of my arrival standing out, and I saw only the normal number of uniformed policemen on duty. I walked up through pleasant gardens to the hotel in ornate Victorian style which overlooked the harbour.

They awaited me in an otherwise deserted, dusty conservatory which I found only after tracking up and down various corridors and many metres of faded carpet.

'You should have entered the hotel as we directed,' said the older of the two old men who sat at a cane table, 'by the way of the lounge bar. In that way you would have been here three minutes earlier and also have avoided the attention of talkative hall porters.'

'I did in fact avoid such notice,' I replied humbly. 'But I am sorry if I have kept you waiting.'

The old fool continued to glare at me. He had a military look about him, with fierce blue eyes. In the lapel of his jacket he wore the tiny rosette of some papal order. The other had a softer, sillier face and was trying to smooth over the disagreement with little smiles and assurances. I let my gaze shift to the third member of the party, a young fellow of about my own age with blond hair and chiselled, if somewhat weak, features, who pretended to be absorbed in the view outside. Against the light I saw that his chin was covered by a light fuzz of beard.

The fierce one broke the silence. He said, 'I trust that you have at last brought news of my flight to Germany.'

'No, general,' hissed the man with the softer, sillier face. 'If you remember, Herr Harris has come on other business.'

'Other business? What business could be more pressing than the offer of five thousand men, many of them seasoned in Spain, ready to lay down their lives to defeat the Bolshevik anti-Christ? An Irish Legion to fight on the Eastern Front, Mr Harris! That is not to be sneezed at, is it?'

'Indeed not, general,' I said.

'All it requires is for myself to fly to Berlin and iron out the ways and means with your general staff.'

'I am sure that your offer is much appreciated and is even now being considered. But as the other officer has said, I come from another department of our government, in pursuit of another matter.'

'This picture pantomime the British will make at Powerscourt?'

The other man answered for me. 'Yes, general.'

The general buried his head in his hands. 'A pantomime,' he groaned theatrically.

'In the Reich,' I said a trifle impatiently, 'a propaganda film may be counted the equal of a division of troops or a fleet of bombers.'

'It was not so when we held the line at Ciempozuelos,' he said, 'against the worst scum of the International Brigade.' He emerged from behind his hands. 'The Bandera Irlanda del Tercio won its glory without the aid of film cameras.'

As far as I remembered from my researches when we were looking for Irish subjects in the Ufa scenario department, the Irish battalion in Spain in fact saw little action and returned home after not more than six months, but it was necessary to humour the old fools.

'Its exploits are still talked of in Germany,' I said.

'Ah yes, we struck up a fine comradeship with the German engineer corps in support on that part of the front. Its commander was Colonel von Thomas. Perhaps you know him.'

'I have heard him speak warmly of the Bandera Irlanda and in particular of your leadership, general.'

'Is that so? I am honoured. Now how may we help you?'

'By introducing him to Powerscourt,' broke in the other.

'Impossible! We do not speak to each other. He is a friend of the British.'

'Not Powerscourt himself. His estate, where the filming will take place.'

'Ah.'

A small cough came from the young fellow who had so far occupied himself with the view. He said, 'If I might pass on the latest progress we have made in this matter . . . '

'What's that?' said the general, swivelling his head. 'Ah, young Dominic. Of course. Carry on.'

Dominic turned pale eyes in my direction without actually meeting my gaze. His voice was clipped in a rather English manner, I thought. He said, 'Lord Powerscourt is the so-called Commissioner for the Boy Scouts in Ireland. You know what is meant by Boy Scouts?'

I nodded impatiently. 'Yes!'

'Every year they hold their camp in the grounds of Powerscourt House. There are permanent cookhouses and so forth. The film company will make use of these installations, and they will stage their battle in the parkland.'

The general snorted.

'Unfortunately, the estate is bounded by walls, and we hear that guards are to be placed at all the gates to keep out strangers.'

'That sounds no great obstacle,' I said. 'But I was not planning to sneak in like a spy. The whole idea was to find me one of the jobs that are created whenever a film unit goes on location – as a cook, perhaps, since you have mentioned cookhouses, or as an extra in the actual filming. If there are battle scenes, they will need plenty of soldiers.'

'I was coming to that,' he said with a hint of petulance. 'The catering has been contracted out to a Dublin firm, Mills's, with whom we have no influence. Some other workers have been taken on, but mostly for unskilled labouring and all of them local men from Enniskerry.'

'The Emergency has brought severe unemployment to our country, Herr Harris,' broke in the soft and silly elder.

'Emergency?' bellowed the general. 'In God's name call it what it is – a war! And a war in which I pray that Irishmen may yet fight!'

After a moment's silence Dominic resumed. 'As for film extras, yes, you are right. At least five hundred are required to act as the English foot-soldiers at the Battle of Agincourt.' He paused.

'If nothing better can be found, I guess that will do,' I said.

'The film company has taken the easy course and recruited existing companies of soldiers.'

I stared at him. 'What do you mean?'

'They are using our Local Defence Volunteers, a part-time militia raised to defend the Free State against invaders – '

'The LDV?' cried the general. 'That rabble would have its work cut out to defend the Free State against a Sunday-school outing.'

I said to Dominic, 'What you have told me so far is not encouraging.'

He met my gaze for the first time. I could see some pink satisfaction glinting in his pale eyes. He demanded suddenly, 'Do you ride?'

'Naturally.'

'Also required are horsemen to ride as the French cavalry. Not so many, perhaps two hundred. And each must bring his own mount.' He waited.

'Go on.'

'All sorts have been volunteering, from the sons of fine houses to poor farm boys.'

'And?'

'My father has some acquaintance with the fellow who is recruiting the riders. We can take our chance.'

'Now you are speaking!'

'There is one other thing.'

'What is that?'

'Everyone has to grow a beard. You will be late starting.'

I felt my chin. Stubble, with me, grew quickly and black. 'I'll catch you up,' I said. Just now I wanted to get away from these dusty old men in this dead, dusty room.

Four

We rode into Enniskerry as cowboys riding into town in a Western movie. Normally, Dominic had told me, this small town less than twenty miles south of Dublin was as sleepy and deserted as a country village. Today the street was thronged with men on horseback. Others held their horses' reins as they stood talking, and drinking from bottles they passed among themselves. They were an assorted bunch, ranging from swarthy fellows who might have been gipsies to quite aristocratic-looking figures. Their attire varied similarly from shapeless jerseys and trousers tucked into rubber boots to well-cut breeches and hacking jackets. On their heads they wore caps or, in one or two cases, felt hats of archaic design. Some of them called in greeting to Dominic.

We had journeyed first to the village of Carrick-mines where Dominic's father ran a small livery stable and Dominic kept his horse. The father was a brusque individual fallen on lean times, I guessed. I learned that he had been an officer in the Irish army supply corps who had resigned his commission in order to join the Spanish adventure. On his return he had been refused reinstatement by the de Valera government. He did not bother to conceal his contempt for the employment we were on our way to seek. 'Try not to get in the way of an arrow,' he sneered to his son.

My mount was to be obtained from a coper in the same vicinity. He was a foxy-faced little ruffian living in a shack who demanded a shamelessly high price for the nondescript roan mare on offer. 'Could I not sell her a hundred times over wid them wanting horses for the fillum?' he kept chanting. We settled for what was still a high price but with an old saddle and harness thrown in. Shoona, as I should call her, carried me comfortably, if sedately, the remainder of the journey.

The first necessity, Dominic muttered, was to find the acquaintance of his father's who was in charge of recruiting the horsemen, and buy him a drink in order to register our presence.

We looked in the hotel, a modest building with small gables above a white-washed façade. Inside, the rooms were dense with smoke and loud voices. We tried another place where a man with a squint said to see if he wasn't at Prosser's. We pushed our way into Prosser's Select Bar and there he was, holding court, a bluff fellow addressed by everyone as 'Master'.

'If it isn't the captain's boy,' he bellowed to Dominic, and insisted on buying us the drink rather than the other way about.

Thirsty after the ride, I tasted my first glass of the black stout I had so often seen my father consume. It was smooth and wholesome. As I tilted the glass a second time, I became aware of a dapper fellow eyeing me.

'You got here then?' he said cheerfully.

Who could he be? What could he mean? My mind raced over the possibilities. Was it some dolt from the Embassy? But no, he spoke English as an Englishman. 'We have arrived by horse,' I said, playing for time.

'Of course they have arrived by bloody horse,' boomed the Master. 'They are my last two flowers of French chivalry who will ride armed and caparisoned against the bowmen of England.'

'Pity,' said the dapper man, still staring at me. 'We could do with a few your height among the bowmen of England. What's your name again?'

'Harris,' I said. 'Frederick Harris.'

'You're not a photographer?'

'I can take photographs. Why do you ask?'

'He is Mr Dallas Bower,' said the Master. 'Assistant producer of the film.'

'I am at your service in any capacity,' I said.

They both looked a little astonished at such a declaration.

'Actually,' said this Bower, 'It's associate producer, not assistant.'

'And what kind of difference would that be?' said the Master.

I bit back the impulse to explain.

Bower said cheerfully, 'The assistant producer is the man who makes all the mistakes, the associate producer is the one who takes the blame.' He looked at me again. 'And didn't I see you at the Ministry?'

Now I really had a turn in my stomach. What else

did he know? I must have betrayed some confusion because he added, 'The Ministry of Information? When you came to seek accreditation?'

Saved again! I knew all about that organization, of course. In the Promi we followed its exploits closely, often with scorn, sometimes with respect. I said, 'No, I have been in Ireland since the war began – '

'The Emergency, you mean,' roared the Master. 'We call it the Emergency.'

I had already encountered this term with the old Blueshirts and knew that he was mocking the fad. 'Of course,' I said gravely. 'Just as we French knights must prepare to meet the English in an emergency.' And so on in similar vein.

'Did you have to make those stupid jokes about Ireland?' said Dominic disapprovingly as soon as we were on our own again.

'The closer one can keep to one's natural disposition,' I quoted from Friedenthal teachings, 'the easier it is to sustain an assumed identity.'

The Powerscourt estate lay quite close to Enniskerry. We had been told not to use the main entrance, a stone portal through which we could see a long avenue bordered by trees, many of fantastic shape, but to work our way round to another gate which led directly to the 'lines', as they would have been termed in the stories of soldiering in India and Africa I had heard from my father. Row upon row of small tents stretched across the field, with larger marquees to serve as stores and a commissary. The aroma of simmering meat and potatoes came from the cookhouse. One tent was marked with a red cross.

Our horses fed and watered and tethered in their own lines, Dominic and I drew blankets and groundsheets and cotton palliasses which we filled with straw, and staked ourselves places in a tent at the far corner of the camp. The ground seemed rather damp here, but Dominic reckoned it might be a little quieter. And so it proved, at least at first.

We talked for a while. Nothing he said changed the impression I had formed on the journey that he was a typical specimen of the 'idealist' brought up to believe that privilege and position were his due, only to find that mucking out his father's stables was all he could command. From such circumstances, I reflected, had come many of the young lions of the Nazi party.

I asked him about the IRA, still not sure whether I might not have been wiser to throw in my lot with them. What was their latest *coup* against the English?

'Two of their officers have taken over a cinema in Belfast and made speeches.' He sounded rather sarcastic.

'Belfast is of course in English territory.'

'In the six counties, yes.'

'You should not despise propaganda if it is effective propaganda.'

'In this case, few will have learned of it. The British press was not allowed to report the incident. Only those who listen into "Lord Haw-Haw" on the German radio heard news of it.'

'That is quite a lot. He has a considerable audience.'

'You know him?'

'I have met him. He is a compatriot of yours. His name is William Joyce.'

'Our hero,' he said, sarcastically again. I wondered just how deeply Dominic was committed to his cause.

The rain began to patter on the tent, and a little later revellers returning from the town tripped over the guy ropes. Curses, drunken songs and arguments could be heard all round. Finally, into the tent itself crashed four unsteady farm boys who exclaimed and swore among themselves in barbaric accents as they wrestled with their boots or attempted to make their beds. One of them dropped the hurricane lamp while attempting to light it, so that the smell of paraffin mixed with the fumes of alcohol and the stench of unwashed feet. Another went only just outside the tent to urinate. Dominic protested in his feeble way and was told to do unmentionable things to himself. I was tempted to practice some of the unarmed combat I had learned at Friedenthal, but was now firmly on guard against drawing attention to myself.

When eventually there was peace, except for drunken snores, I lay listening to the rain on the canvas and was transported back to the camps I had attended as a member first of the *Jungvolk* and later the *Hitler Jugend*, until the life of the studios poisoned my enthusiasm. How we had drilled and marched and sung in the fresh air of lakes and woodland! How good the sausage and potatoes had tasted! For nearly four years of war I had secretly hankered for the camaraderie of the soldier's life. How ironic that I should experience it, at last, among lumpish mercenaries hired to pretend a battle.

In the hours before dawn the rain grew heavier. The farmers awoke, cursing, to find themselves in pools of water and did not return the next night.

It may be imagined with what eagerness and curiosity I awaited the morning parade, to be addressed by Laurence Olivier himself. We assembled on an open space in the parkland below the camp. The rain had stopped, although the sky was still grey and the trees dripped. To one side lay Powerscourt House, an imposing mansion surmounted by copper domes and flanked by smaller buildings. In the other direction the park stretched away to a wooded hill. Large birds circled above it, large enough to be eagles. The hollow ring of metal upon metal came from a lorry, nearer at hand, being unloaded of its cargo of steel scaffolding.

I surveyed the army to which I now belonged. There were nearly two hundred of us horsemen, plus some local defence volunteers who had arrived early in order to learn to handle the bow. The remainder would follow when filming was about to start. The men stood or squatted where they fancied, some puffing at clay pipes, others passing the time by tossing coins in some simple, interminable game. Their beards were well advanced compared to mine, but the word was that it would be a week before the camera started to turn.

At last three or four figures came striding from the direction of the house. Drawing ahead of the others was one who was unmistakably the leader. He stood for a moment, regarding us, until one of the others hurried up with a wooden crate of the kind that holds beer bottles and placed it on the ground. Olivier stepped on to the crate, introduced himself and immediately began to describe the action scenes we had been engaged to take part in. He was of average height, I judged, and athletic of build. His hair was cut in startling fashion, as if a basin had been placed on his head and the clippers applied to all surfaces below. He was elegantly formal in his dress, with a coloured silk scarf tucked into the open neck of his shirt, just as I remembered Esmond Knight sporting at Neubabelsberg.

Though I had placed myself near the front, I am sure his voice would have carried clearly to everyone. He spoke quite conversationally, but every word seemed to breast the air. Only at the end did he raise his voice in exhortation. 'I may be asking you to do some dangerous things in the weeks to come, but I promise you I will not expect you to do anything I won't first undertake myself.'

A moment's silence followed. Olivier stood stock still on his tiny stage as if poised to meet whatever cheers or catcalls should rebound. Then came a curious sound from the company, a kind of growl of acceptance. A single voice called out, 'We'll hold you to that, Mr Olivier.' Olivier smiled and sprang down.

The day passed as the next few days would pass, in various preparations. We had our hair cut in much the same drastic style as that sported by Olivier. We lined up in small groups to be fitted with 'chain mail' knitted from heavy twine before being sprayed with metallic paint. Blind students, said the costume assistant wryly, had been hard at work with their needles. The sets of real armour available would be allocated to the riders on the best horses, who would be placed in the forefront of the battle scenes. This did not seem likely to apply to me; although my stolid Shoona did not bear the harness marks that had to be groomed out of the plough horses, she was on the small side and her backbone sagged.

Under the eyes of a grizzled figure said to be formerly a sergeant in an English, or perhaps Scottish, cavalry regiment, we had riding practice with the raised wooden saddles and other trappings or medieval harness. I made a note of what he said, against the possibility of having such a character in *Kolberg*. 'I have seen some unpromising material in my time,' he told us, 'but you lot is in a class by yourselves.' Yet the bandy-legged peasants seemed to adopt themselves effortlessly while I felt no less insecure. Either Shoona was unresponsive and the others brushed past us as they forced their way ahead, or she would suddenly take it upon herself to break into a shambling gallop and all my energies had to be concentrated on trying to hang on.

At the end of the first day I went with Dominic to the 'wet canteen' or bar that had been opened for the company – rashly, one might have supposed, but this night it was quiet. Dominic guessed that many of the men had spent the payment they had been given in advance and would now have to wait for their first weekly wage. Some of those who were present whiled away the time tossing pennies against one another. Others listened to a radio set.

As we sipped our porter, I felt daunted by the enormity of the task set me. Merely to come face to face with Olivier was going to be hellishly difficult. Remembering my own studio days, when sooner or later one had a message for the greatest stars on the lot, I had assumed there would be the same ease of approach here. I had forgotten that the messenger enjoys a privileged role. Here it was much more like the army life we were busy pretending. I was one of the hundreds in the ranks, Olivier was the King.

If I did succeed in confronting him, would he agree? It looked an ever remoter possibility. If we had to abduct him, how much support could I count on from our mercenary Irish 'allies'? Could even the strong arm of the Reich stretch this far to play its part?

People were gathering around the radio for the news bulletin.

'What day is this?' I demanded of Dominic.

'Tuesday.'

'The date?'

'The first of June.'

'Let us listen.'

The second item was that German fighters had intercepted and shot down a civilian airliner flying from Lisbon to England. Among the seventeen on board had been the actor Leslie Howard. I reproached myself for my faint heart of only a few minutes earlier.

Five

Already the English camp at Agincourt was taking shape, little white tents like minarets standing out crisply in the damp Irish air. The French camp was situated on the slope of a low hill, perhaps a kilometre and a half away. It had fine pavilions of blue and gold fabric, with banners and pennants. Between the two camps lay the long stretch of parkland over which the battle would be fought.

I was drawn by the sound of metal upon metal to where, at one side, the camera track was being laid for the charge. It ran parallel to a narrow estate road until the road curved inwards and the track crossed it. Behind the road workmen were uprooting an iron fence where it might intrude into the shot. Others were driving spikes into the ground to complete the track itself.

I approached casually, hands in pockets. As I had suspected, it was a markedly inferior piece of work by the standards of German film-making. The sleepers were sound enough, but the 'rails' were no more than lengths of tubular scaffolding joined with clamps. It would be bumpy and at the same time too slippery. Iron wheels would not grip the rounded surface. In 1941 I had been on location for Veit Harlan's *The Great King*. The track for one of the battle sequences had been made from the rails of a light mineral railway and even on this the wheels of the camera car slipped and raced.

'So what do you think of it?'

I spun round, startled. I had been so immersed I had not heard anyone approach.

It was the associate producer Bower whom I had met as we arrived in Enniskerry that first day.

I said, 'You could not find proper rails?'

'Not for love nor money.'

It was on the tip of my tongue to tell him of the troubles I foresaw, but an instinct held me back. 'It is most ingenious,' I said lamely.

'It is certainly that.' He was already continuing on his way.

How stupid of me! Here was the means of getting closer to Olivier, through his right-hand man, and I was throwing it away.

I called after him, 'I think I remember where we met.'

He replied, scarcely bothering to turn, 'No, no, old boy. It was all a mistake. I confused you with this young chap who wants to come and take photographs.'

'I can use a camera,' I cried again. But he walked on.

The next day I made sure of watching the first tests of the camera car. An old sedan, which I recognized as a V-8 Ford, had been stripped of much of its bodywork and fitted with a wooden

platform for the camera. The tyres had been removed from the wheels so that the rims ran directly
on the tubular tracks.

While they fussed over preliminary expeditions
and adjustments, I took the opportunity of identi-
fying as many as I could of those present. I had
studied the call sheets pinned up each evening
which indicated who was required next day, and
made note of certain names. The small, slim man of
some thirty years of age who stood on the camera
platform and called out in an accent strange to my
ears could only be Robert Krasker, the cinematographer. His name was known in the filmworld: he
was an Australian, it now came to me, who had
studied at Dresden and worked in Paris before
moving to London.

The younger man with him had to be J. Hildyard,
who would be actually operating the camera, which
was much larger and more cumbersome than anything I had previously seen. It conformed, of course,
to the American Technicolor system which demanded three separate negatives. What I did not yet
know was that it was the only such instrument in
Europe, a fact which perhaps explained the anxious
expression on the face of the third figure on the
camera platform. He was George Menassian, an
American and an employee of the Technicolor
company.

I could not place the man driving the car but he
looked too elegant to be a mere film tradesman. The
mechanic who hovered in attendance, on the other
hand, was clearly a local artisan.

Now came a test along the full length of the track,

with horsemen to set the required pace. They cantered away up the field towards a clump of trees at the far end. The car followed them slowly in reverse, engine whining.

Among the onlookers near me was Dallas Bower, with a whistle suspended from a lanyard round his neck and stop-watch in his hand. He blew the whistle and waved.

The rig started back towards us, slowly at first, accelerating as the horsemen following them on their left changed from a walk into a jog. I could see Krasker and Hildyard, tiny figures crouched over the camera. Above the din from the wheels came another noise, that of the V-8 engine racing and subsiding, then racing and subsiding again. The horsemen were already having to reign back as they broke into a canter and then a gallop. They thudded up well ahead of the vehicle that was supposed to keep abreast of them.

'Congratulations, you have won!'

The voice rang out sardonically from behind me. I spun round to see Olivier astride a magnificent white horse.

'That we couldn't help at all, Mr Olivier,' said the leading horseman. 'Every time the people in the car had to go faster they went slower, if you follow me.'

'Not your fault, Paddy. So what went wrong, Bob?'

Krasker shrugged. 'It's useless. It won't do. The camera's shaking like a dog and the wheels just slip when Paul tries to accelerate.'

'All right. What do we do next?'

A fellow who was evidently the grip, as the

76

tradesman who looks after the camera track is called, muttered something about roughing the tubular pipes to give better purchase for the wheels.

'Christ, it's too rough already,' said Krasker.

The driver who had been referred to as Paul asked if some sort of rubber collar could not be fitted to each wheel – not a tyre but something just thick enough to cushion the ride a small amount and also improve adhesion.

The grip exchanged glances with the mechanic. The mechanic scratched his head and said that to be sure, they could have a try.

'By this time tomorrow,' cried Olivier, and wheeled his horse away before I could attract his attention. But that was the whole task – to catch the great man's eye.

That evening the call sheet posted in the canteen announced the first turning of the camera. A hundred of us horsemen were called. A detailed time-table for accoutring, make-up, etcetera, was given, beginning with an item that I had never seen in filming schedules before.

'What does it mean by Mass, in the canteen tent?' I asked Dominic.

'What it says. Mass in the canteen tent.'

'Who will attend?'

'I shall, for one,' he said frostily.

'And many others?'

'Do not forget we are a priest-ridden country,' he said sarcastically.

Next morning, hastening from the 'ablutions' or wash-house, I took a peep into the tent as I passed.

It was crowded. Quite a few of last night's drunkards and roisterers were now crouched in prayer.

We groomed our horses and put a final polish to harness and saddlery. We waited in line to draw our costumes and accoutrements. As a proficient rider with a good mount, Dominic was cast as a knight with a proper helmet and vizor and plumes. He carried a lance and a shield emblazoned with leopards. I was to be a mere squire, or less, armed with an axe and protected only by a tunic of the improvised chain mail. My helmet was like a shallow bowl atop my head. Leaving my face exposed, it ruled out any possibility of wearing glasses. In addition to everything else I should be half-blind!

It also meant that I was one of those ordered to have make-up, even though I was unlikely to stray within a hundred metres of the camera. Again I waited my turn. There were but three girls. Two of them were typical of the young Heidis and Gretchens to be found in the make-up rooms at the Ufastadt. Their hair was combed and pinned up in the fashion which seemed to span all frontiers – one could see it in Berlin and Paris and the latest Hollywood film. They chattered to each other with many giggles.

The third was different. She was tall and rather fine-looking, her fair hair in the page-boy style. She spoke rarely, but worked with a frown of concentration and quick movements of her slender hands.

It was in her chair that I made sure I sat.

'I am sorry to inflict such a mug on you,' I said humorously.

She made only some little noise which could be

interpreted at will, and began at once to apply some liquid of darkish hue. She used a small sponge but also the tips of her fingers on my eyelids and the corners of my mouth.

'So you give me a sun tan,' I tried again.

'No, just the stains of battle.' Her voice was refined and girlish, like that of the English actress Nova Pilbeam I had seen in one or perhaps two films. She reached for a powder puff.

'Perhaps you will have Mr Olivier next. That will give you better material, eh?'

'He's not called today.' She was dusting on the powder.

'But when he is to be made up, I guess it is you he asks for.'

'Sometimes.' Now she whisked a soft brush over her handiwork.

'Then I shall demand you, too! What is your name?'

Instead of replying, she said, 'Please keep your mouth closed a moment.' With scissors she snipped deftly at stray ends of my beard. All too soon she was undoing the sheet she had tied under my chin.

'You will do,' she said.

As we assembled in rough formation, Olivier and the cavalry sergeant and the Master rode through the ranks to inspect their flower of French chivalry.

I escaped attention thanks to the presence close by of some of the least soldierly of the Irish. Several of them slumped in their saddles like so many sacks of potatoes. The evil, tiny man next to me perched like a monkey on his steed, his stirrups so high that his knees were bent sharply forward.

'He looks like a jockey,' I heard Olivier cry.

'He *is* a jockey,' came the Master's voice. 'I've told him about those stirrups.'

Yet I could not escape a tingle in the blood as the foremost riders moved off to take up position. I had grown up among the pretence of the studios. All around was the familiar litter of a unit on location: a shooting-brake with its rear doors open, a trestle table bearing a Thermos container of coffee, cables snaking everywhere.

I still found myself seized by the crazy five-per-cent illusion that it was all real. The farm horses and hacks which had looked so ordinary now picked their way with high proud steps. Their heads were masked and their bodies draped. The metal of their trappings clinked and chinked and winked in the sun. The riders had been even more dramatically transformed with gleaming armour, plumes, fierce snouty helmets. They carried shields and banners emblazoned with blue and gold and crimson designs. The sullen Dominic was no longer Dominic, but a young knight who had ridden from Aquitaine to do battle for his King.

The spell was soon punctured, of course, by the fits and starts of actual filming. On the surface it was a straightforward set-up. Four troops of horsemen breast the brow of a low hill and ride on towards camera in echelon – in the finished movie it comes some time after the charge and the first clash of the armies, when the battle has been divided, scattered into separate skirmishes. The shot lasts maybe ten seconds of screen time. But today it took much marshalling and remarshalling. Olivier would gallop up on his white steed, megaphone in hand, and then gallop back to the camera position. Our manoeuvre would be too slow or too fast or too ragged. If we got it right, there would be distant onlookers straying into shot, or the take would be called off because a cloud dimmed the light. Each time we were cued I had to steel myself afresh, for as the misfit of the rearguard I was cursed whenever anything went wrong.

'Jesus, you'll have us here till midnight,' hissed the vile little jockey.

Also, my stirrups must have been too short, and my long legs pushed me back against the raised cantle. I felt it chafing against the skin of my back.

At last the signal came that they were satisfied. The film had written its first sentence.

The saddle had rubbed a raw place towards the base of my spine, in the cleft of the buttocks. My shirt tail was stained with blood. 'What should I do?' I asked Dominic.

He put on his most sulky manner. 'Do you have to stick your horrible bum in my face? It is nothing.'

'Such abrasions can easily become infected.'

'Then go to the first-aid tent.'

There the nurse cleaned the place with spirit and fixed a lint dressing with sticking plaster. 'Just as well to have it seen to,' she said.

When I returned to our tent Dominic was lying on his bed. He thrust something between the bed-clothes.

'So what is that you hide?' I snapped.

'Nothing.'

We had built our beds up on crates against the wet ground. I reached down and tipped his over on its side so that he tumbled off, swearing.

It was nothing but a naturist magazine, smudgily printed and with its naked persons deprived of their sexual organs by the retoucher's brush. 'In Germany at least we do not mutilate the subjects,' I said. 'But why did you want to conceal it? We are all flesh and blood.'

He muttered something about such publications being banned in the Free State and he had to protect the fellow who lent him this copy.

'It is Saturday,' I said. 'The nurse in the first-aid tent says there is a dance tonight in the Legion Hall.'

'Everyone knows that.'

'We shall go.'

'Is that safe? For you, I mean?'

'As safe as skulking around here.'

'The policeman will look in, for sure!'

'The policeman! Some peasant crammed into a uniform.'

He said, 'It will hardly be a select occasion, you know.'

'There will be women. And who knows – Olivier may attend. The nurse was full of it. That could be useful.'

'It could also attract the attention of another class of policeman altogether.'

'Who do you mean?'

'The Special Branch, our Irish Gestapo.'

'In which case we can memorize their apperance.'

But what sighs and sulks before we could be on our way. I put on the best jacket I had brought with me. Dominic swore and demanded, 'What is that meant to be?'

'It is not meant to be anything, it is my jacket.'

'That little belt thing at the back. And look at those ridiculous pleats in the pockets – you might as well wear jack-boots and shout "Heil Hitler!" '

He grumbled again at the two- or three-mile walk to the Legion Hall. For my part, I enjoyed stepping out in the mild air. It was a fine evening, the last for many a day as things turned out. On the road, several jaunting carts, as they are called, overtook us with members of the film unit aboard. I recognized Hildyard from the camera crew, and sitting next to him, in the sideways arrangement of these small carriages, one of the make-up artists. I wondered if my tall goddess would be there.

Our destination announced itself first with the noise of music. Inside, only a few couples were dancing but around the floor the crowd was dense, the men to one side – the girls to the other. Already the tobacco smoke eddied in the rays from the rather poor electric lights suspended from the rafters.

'Come on, we'll have something to drink,' I said. When we had succeeded in pushing our way to the bar, we stood with our glasses among the peasants and farm boys who looked on. I lit a pipe and was content, for the moment, to listen to the band. Its attempts at dance music in the American-Jewish idiom were pretty laughable, but every so often the banjo would be laid aside and the fiddle taken up, and a batch of tunes with an Irish lilt to them would follow. At these times the local girls took the floor and danced among themselves, with their hands at their sides and their feet executing the most dainty steps.

'Are you not going to dance?' I asked Dominic. 'Look at the beautiful young creatures just waiting for you to invite them.' To tell the truth, I was becoming bored with the way he clung to me or kept watch over me, whichever it was, and would have welcomed his departure on to the floor; but he only gave a snort of disdain.

It was at this moment that I spied my tall goddess of the make-up table. She stood on the edge of the crowd on the women's side, with a girl I recognized as the continuity aide. 'Well then, I shall,' I snapped, and made my way through the throng.

She did not recognize me at once. So many bristly faces would have presented themselves for her attentions, how could she? I still felt a small pang of disappointment.

'You never did tell me your name,' I said as I led her on to the floor.

'You'll only laugh.'

'I will not.'

'Or start singing it. Everybody does.'

'I promise I will do neither.'

We danced for a short while before she spoke again. She held herself very straight and at a little distance from me, but moved so lightly.

'All right,' she said at last. 'It's Angeline. Angeline Byers.'

'But that is a beautiful and surely unusual name.'

'It was until the song.'

'Ah yes.' I had to be careful. 'How did it go again?'

'She danced all day on the village green' – she did not sing this at all, but spat it out flatly – 'poo-oor little Angeline. I could have murdered her.'

I gave the hand in mine a sympathetic squeeze. 'I will do it for you.'

'You may have to tonight, if they have a "Palais Glide". And what is yours?'

'My name? Harris. Frederick Harris.' I could think of nothing amusing with which to embroider that. But gradually she began to relax in my arms. I found enough to keep her attentive during the pause between dances so that we embarked upon a second one quite naturally. Perhaps she was relieved, being a young woman who would have towered over any of the Irishmen, to find a partner who was taller.

As I sensed, she was a cut above the flibbertigib-bets who were so often attracted to jobs in the film studios. Her father was employed by the Cable & Wireless Company and much of her childhood had been spent overseas. She had been for one year to art school before starting work.

'When the war is over I shall go back,' she said.

'For me, the cinema.'

We talked, of course, of this film of *Henry V*. 'What is it about, apart from a battle?' I said. 'I am ashamed that I do not know.'

'No good asking me,' she said. 'We did *Julius Caesar* for School Cert. Joan would know. Ask her.'

Joan was the continuity girl with whom she had arrived. I bought them both a drink of gin with orange juice. Joan also nearly caught me out by saying she had a Penguin I might borrow if I liked.

'A penguin?'

'A Penguin book. The text of the play.'

'Excuse me, I am stupid tonight. That would be kind.'

I danced once more with her, as politeness dictated, then reclaimed Angeline. This time she relaxed still more, smiling with me at some of the shuffling couples we encountered. Once, the lights were dimmed so that a spotlight could pick out a couple at random when the music stopped. For the man there was a small paper packet of cigarettes, for the girl some hairclips; and for me, in the shadows, the best prize of all as I kept hold of Angeline's hand and let my face be brushed by her silky hair.

It was just after this that Olivier paid his visit. Oh, the excitement! All the girls squealed and some pressed forward to try and touch him. Even Angeline, I couldn't help noticing, stared with shining eyes and lips parted as he made his progress across the floor and sprang on to the little stage with the band. The drummer beat a roll on his drums. Olivier spoke.

He looked every inch the film star, with a patterned cravat at his neck again, a handsome jacket, his face tanned from the days in the open, his eyes flashing and humorous. He said how grateful he and the unit were to the people of Ireland, and of Enniskerry in particular, for their hospitality. And how pretty were the girls of Enniskerry, which brought renewed squeals from those demoiselles.

When his voice took on a ringing tone and he began to talk again of the battle scenes to be fought, I let my gaze wander to his entourage. Dallas Bower was there, also the fellow who had been at the wheel of the camera car during the test runs. Paul, they had called him. With him was a young woman. Who were they, I asked softly to Angeline. She whispered back that they were the art director and his assistant. Ah, so . . .

But what about the two men who stood a little apart, still wearing their raincoats and hats – the older one a billycock, the younger a soft fedora? It was not difficult to guess they might be the secret policemen or 'Special Branch', spoken of by Dominic. When one of them looked hard in my direction, I had a foolish urge to duck away.

Olivier finished his peroration. The crowd clapped and whistled as with a last seigneurial wave he led his party away. It was now or never if I were to use this opportunity to come face to face with him. I muttered to Angeline, 'I will be back in a moment,' and hurried after them. Needless to say, shrill girls impeded my path. I pushed my way through them at last and emerged into the evening air. There was no sign of them, but, as I peered into the gloom, rough arms pinioned mine, a hood was pulled over my head and I was bundled into a waiting car.

Two figures came slowly into focus when, after a journey of perhaps three quarters of an hour followed by some fifty paces of frog-marching, the hood was jerked from my head. I was in a small kitchen, as of a modest house. I blinked in the harsh light of an unshaded electric globe.

The two men sat at a table on which reposed a teapot and cracked cups, a bottle of stout and a bottle of whiskey. One was a large fellow with a red

87

face and sandy hair, the other a dark man with narrow features, unblinking eyes and an air of authority. After some grunted questions intended to establish that I was indeed named Harris, and which any fool could have satisfied, the large one asked in sarcastic tones if my journey had been comfortable.

'Apart from the attentions of these gentlemen,' I snapped, jerking my arms in the grip of the two others who had brought me and still held me.

'Let him go,' said the dark man quietly. He watched me rub my elbows and flex my fingers before adding, 'My colleague was referring to the fishing vessel which landed you in our country.'

That was a cunning opening shot, but I managed to contrive a look of puzzlement. 'Fishing vessel?'

'Jesus!' roared the red-faced man. 'There were enough poor souls whose noses were filled wid the stink when you took the bus to Cork.'

'I don't know what you talk of,' I said.

The authoritative man spoke again. 'The boat was called the *Philomena*,' he said conversationally. 'She made rendezvous with the U-608 forty miles off Fastnet and put into Youghal two nights later, on 17 May. We know all this because we organized it.'

Now I was flummoxed.

'Which was not easy,' bellowed Red-Face, 'bearing in mind that another of your submarines had sunk the *Irish Oak* not a week and a half before. Irishmen drowned!' He gave the word a thickness that made it sound like 'throwned'.

'All right, that will do,' said the dark man. 'Such things happen in war. But it is true that persuading the necessary people was more difficult than usual, and lining the necessary pockets more costly. So you may imagine that we were not a little surprised when you failed to contact us on your arrival in Dublin.'

Was it a trap? But if they knew all this they would know the rest.

'I guess you are of the IRA,' I said.

The dark man nodded.

'I am sorry,' I said. 'The Embassy sent me to the others.'

'That we also know, Mr Harris. We know pretty well all you have done since your meeting with Petersen, which would have attracted the attention of a blind man with a hearing trumpet. Perhaps we are lucky that you did not try to seek us out.'

I let that pass. If they were to drive me back without further ado I might just regain the dance before it finished. 'Very well,' I said. 'If I find I need your help, I shall contact you. Now if you would – '

'But not by the telephone, Mr Harris,' said the dark man softly. 'And especially not if you have to shout at the operator and generally advertise the number you desire, as you did when ringing your embassy.'

'Button B did not return any of the twopences I put in.'

'It is the children. They block the aperture with wads of paper. Then they come back, take away the paper and receive a harvest of coins.'

'I have done it myself,' said the red-faced man.

'Now, tell us, please,' said the dark man, 'exactly what you have come to do.'

I began to explain as concisely as I could, until the red-faced man interrupted. 'A fillum,' he sneered.

'We are to help you maintain yourself among idiots making a fillum? How many British will that kill?'

'If all goes well, none,' I retorted.

'So what is the point, for Jesus, Joseph and Mary's sake?'

I did not feel inclined to try and pass on to him the fine aims of Reich propaganda. 'Leave the point to us,' I snapped.

'There is just one other matter,' said the dark man. 'The question of remuneration.'

'That may be settled only when we know what I ask of you.'

'A little something on account?'

I looked at my watch again. 'Twenty pounds.'

'Twenty-five.'

'Very well.'

'In sovereigns?' demanded the red-faced one.

'In notes,' I said firmly.

The car seemed to crawl back. Twice on the way the red-faced man, who was now driving, wished to stop at public houses though it was now after the time they were required by law to close. 'They know me round the back,' he said, and I had to promise him as much drink as he could want at the Legion Hall bar if only we were in time. All in vain, for the band had put away its music and, although there were still people drinking and milling about, there was no sign of Angeline, nor indeed of any of the film unit.

Dominic pretended that he had searched every-where for me. 'I thought the Special Branch must have got you.'

'They were merely protecting Mr Olivier from

squealing girls,' I said.

'What did happen to you then?'

I saw no reason not to tell him.

He frowned. 'They are gangsters.'

I shrugged. 'It may turn out that gangsters have their uses.'

'At least they took you away from that stuck-up girl.' It was almost as if he were jealous.

The episode had taught me two things. Next day I unpacked the 7.65 mm Walther pistol I had brought with me, and from then on kept it on my person or in easy reach. It also forced me to take stock of just how little I knew of this enemy operation – for such it was – I had to penetrate. In one hour of the company of a make-up artist and a continuity girl I had picked up more about the film than in almost one week among the ranks of outsiders whose interests were horses and drink and gambling their money away in the tossing of coins. Where, for example, were members of the unit living, in particular, of course, Olivier? The maidens told me they were in a private hotel, as they termed it. The camera crew were at the hotel in Enniskerry, others in rooms above public houses and so forth. Concerning Olivier, they had no information, but he had arrived, that first morning, from the direction of the great house. Perhaps he was the guest of the nobleman Powerscourt who lived there.

What I had established from Angeline and Joan, as they gossiped about it between themselves, was that he had not brought his wife. The beautiful Vivien Leigh was in North Africa with a soldier-entertainment troupe. Well, that might ease my task. He would be worried about her.

This Sunday was a rest day. While Dominic slept, I set off to spy out the land anew. The one advantage of being a horseman was that, under the pretence of exercising my mount, I could ride freely round the estate. To the watchmen wearing armbands who now guarded all the entrances, I was just another bearded extra lured by the prospect of seventy shillings a week. There was a useful anonymity to it.

From a gardener I gleaned the confirmation that yes, there were three of the gentlemen from the fillum staying in the butler's house, but there was some talk of one of them moving into a caravan. Certainly a caravan had arrived from Kingstown.

As I returned towards camp a tractor was towing a caravan up the field behind the horse lines. I changed course to come upon it. The tractor driver was manoeuvring the caravan into position as I pulled up.

'For Mr Olivier?' I shouted above the clatter of this motor.

'So they tell me. He will be living like General Montgomery in the desert.'

'Or Rommel!' But it was a sour rejoinder for a German to have to make, so soon after we had been driven from Africa.

From within our tent came the sound of voices and laughter. Both ceased as I pushed in. Dominic sat on his bed; a big-boned, red-haired fellow sprawled on mine, mudded riding boots and all. He gave me a nod but made no effort to move.

'This is Fergus Simmons,' said Dominic. 'He rides as the Constable of France when we film the charge.'

'Indeed?' I said coldly.

'And yourself?' asked this Fergus blandly.

'As a poor retainer.'

'Did you hear of that Dublin cabby who brought his poor nag that's more used to dozing between the shafts than galloping? The creature is about as warlike as an old sheep, but the fellow was highly indignant not to be given a place in the ranks of the lordly.'

And so on, all lapped up by Dominic with eager attentiveness until at last Fergus unwound himself of my bed and said he would see Dominic at the site in due course. I waited for Dominic to explain.

'He is a famous rider,' he said at last. 'His family has land in three counties, and hunts with the Blazers.'

'What did he want?'

'We are to pace the camera car when they try it again presently, just a small troop of us. Fergus will be the leader, of course.'

'Ah, so you are singled out. It is an honour?'

He shrugged.

For perhaps ten minutes we went about our separate activities in silence. I pulled off my boots, Dominic pulled his on. When he spoke again it was in a detached tone.

'They have fitted rubber treads on the wheel rims, down at the garage in Enniskerry.'

'It will never work. Veit Harlan had the same problem when he was shooting the Battle of Torgau for *The Great King*. The only thing is to replace the proper tyres, inflated to the correct pressure.'

'That is nonsense. The car would not then stay on

the track for one yard.'

'Curiously, I do know a little of film-making. One merely bolts a kind of flange to each wheel, to run inside the track. It makes a hellish noise but one is never shooting directly on to sound-film on such occasions.

He rose to his feet. 'Are you coming to watch?'

'I feel lazy. You shall tell me all about it.'

I dozed a little and thought sadly about Angeline, until I was forced to rummage among Dominic's baggage and find his stupid naturist magazine in order to distract myself.

He came back full of himself and his tidings. Apparently the camera car had behaved perfectly well at first. As he described it, circlets of solid rubber had been wrapped round the rims of the wheels. The ride was immediately much smoother as it reversed up to the head of the track. Krasker had been quite jubilant, raising his cocked thumb in the air to signify optimism.

As they began the acceleration of the charge, however, they heard again the engine beginning to race, and saw wisps of smoke from the wheels. By full gallop the wisps had become streams, and as the car pulled up it was enveloped in a greasy cloud. The grip had leaped forward with a fire extinguisher, but in fact the rubber was already burned away to nothing.

'Good,' I said.

'Now they will try the tyres and flanges.'

'How did they know about that?'

He hesitated.

'Did you tell them?'

'Of course not, but . . . '

'But what, idiot?'

'I had been talking to Fergus Simmons about it, and he must have said something.'

I gave him a shove that sent him on his back. 'Arse-head! Whose side are you on?'

He stared up at me uncomprehendingly.

'We are not here to help the English!'

'You didn't say so,' he whined. 'I thought you meant me to pass on the tip. Why else did you mention it?'

There was perhaps a grain of truth in that. It was difficult, coming from the filmworld, not to identify oneself with any film on which one worked. But from now on there was to be no confusion. Everything had to go wrong for Olivier, so that he would become more and more downhearted. Then, and only then, might our proposals have an attraction.

The first opportunity to put this philosophy into practice came as we were rehearsing a scene in which English soldiers were to drop from the trees on to horsemen passing below and drag them to the ground. Olivier himself explained exactly what he wanted and how it should be done.

'You there' – to those of us who were to be the monkeys in the trees – 'you are perching on the branches. All right? Hold on firmly with your hands. As the horseman approaches, push your feet away, hang on for a second and then let go, pull him from the horse and the two of you drop nice and easily to the ground. Is that clear?'

I remembered his assurance that he would not ask

us to do anything he was not willing to do himself.

From the back of the group of us, in my best Irish brogue, I called out, 'Would you mind showing us exactly how you mean, Mr Oliver?' – all the peasants pronounced his name thus.

There was a rumble of agreement. Olivier's response was to hold out his hand and be hoisted into the trees by those around him. I guess the branch was about six metres up. He crouched rather precariously with his hands between his feet, gripping the branch, and – it seemed – slipped rather than launched himself off. He hung by his hands for perhaps a second then dropped heavily to the ground. I saw him wince. He staggered, and clutched the tree-trunk.

'There you are,' he cried rather desperately. 'Nothing to it.'

From my parachute drop at Friedenthal I had a fair idea of the signs of a ruined ankle. I was not wrong. The next day Olivier appeared not merely with a stick but hobbling on a crutch!

In addition to this, the weather was now relentlessly hostile. It rained for sometimes the whole day. If the rain stopped, the sun still did not shine, and sunlight was necessary for the Technicolor camera. If the sun did emerge, the rain clouds would pile up again before any ambitious scene could be set up.

As for the camera car, I could not see it ever functioning properly on that crazy track. 'The Battle of Agincourt will not take place,' I told Dominic, though of course he did not catch the allusion to the play *La Guerre de Troie n'aura pas lieu* of Jean Giradoux. It had lain around the scenario department at Ufa when someone – von Baky, perhaps – had a notion to adapt it.

The one drawback to all these circumstances was that with scarcely any filming being done there was therefore no call for the make-up department. I loitered in vain around the stores and location office for a glimpse of Angeline.

Eventually, after some three or four days had passed, I contrived to come face to face with the continuity girl Joan.

'Oh, it's you!' she said with a stern look, but agreed to deliver a letter for me.

I waited anxiously for a reply. When none came, I sought out Joan again.

Yes, yes, she said, as if that were the whole of the matter, she had given the letter to Angeline.

And did she have nothing for me in return?

She stared at me blankly, then exclaimed that she would forget her own head next. She rummaged in her handbag. I held out my hand eagerly. Alas, it was only the small paperbound copy of the text of *Henry V* she had promised.

Six

The foot soldiers arrived for the big battle sequences. Most of them, as Dominic had forecast, were from the Local Defence force recruited to drive out any invading Germans or – more likely – English. I did not think either enemy would be long impeded by this army, but its soldiers took themselves seriously and paraded each morning to a bugle. For two nights we had half a dozen in our tent, until the rain washed them out again.

One day Dominic and I watched the bowmen at practice. Those who had come early and were now proficient would occupy the foreground in their scenes, but all had to look skilled. It was necessary to exert great strength to draw the bow, which was nearly as long as a man is tall.

These fellows had become quite absorbed in it. They had set up a target of straw bales eighty or a hundred metres away, and from the boastful talk of the havoc their arrows were going to cause among the French, you would have thought they were real archers preparing for a real battle. Perhaps it was just as well they did not often hit the target.

'May we have a try?' I called to them, ignoring Dominic's snarls to be quiet.

They let us do just that, with much enjoyment of our clumsy efforts. Dominic soon gave up, scowling. I persevered.

One man showed me honestly the knack of almost climbing inside the bow to draw it, the correct grip with the fingers of the right hand and how the shaft should rest on the bent thumb of the left. After further misfires and a painful sting across my forearm from the string, I thwacked a couple of arrows into the bales and, while everyone cheered ironically, a third one for good measure.

It was satisfying to better Dominic in one physical pursuit, even if rehearsals for the great charge soon reduced me once more to the clown squad. The best riders were chosen to represent named characters such as the Constable, the Dauphin and the Duke of Orleans. The most reliable of the remainder were placed at the far end of the front rank, where the task of keeping a fine straight line of advancing knights on horseback would be most difficult.

Dominic had his place there. I was stowed away, needless to say, in the rear rank at the near end, among the stupidest of the farm hands and stable lads. They continually grumbled about the need to rehearse at all, believing that all that was necessary was to point their horse in approximately the right direction and hack it in the ribs.

The film plan, evidently, was that at the beginning of the charge the camera should be well forward of the line of horsemen, shooting directly backwards. As we gained speed it would slowly pan along the ranks until – towards the end of the track – we would be level with the car and then thundering past.

Each time we tried this there was a span of a few seconds when I found myself running quite close to the camera car. If, against all expectations, a take did seem to be going too well, it should not be impossible to veer off course and mask the camera at a crucial moment, or something of that nature.

I spent that evening immersed in the paper book of *Henry V*. A shooting script would have been better, because nowhere in the text could I find any directions for a charge of the French cavalry. Perhaps this was not possible in the playhouse of Shakespeare's time. There was a character in his text called Chorus, whose only task was to introduce the events of the play with elaborate apologies for the shortcomings of the theatre when it came to presenting battle scenes, etcetera.

I had every intention that his words should apply equally to the cinema.

Next day, and whenever in ensuing days I could escape Dominic's suspicious stare, I sought out my new acquaintances the bowmen. I would practice again with them, becoming more and more proficient. Their instructor was an Anglo-Irishman who had competed in archery contests. At my urging he brought along some bows of his own making.

'Would you sell me one?' I demanded.

He was surprised, but I flattered him with some nonsense, and perhaps he was glad of the gold sovereign. It was not difficult to 'lose' – and thus acquire – a couple of fine steel-tipped arrows. One could never be sure what skill might not be useful in the crazy filmwar.

At last the skies cleared. Filming would resume at once, first a day of preparatory shots and then, if all went well, the charge. I was filled with an excitement and apprehension I had not felt since adolescence, when the next day might bring the chance of seeing some impossibly loved one.

Yes! Angeline was at her make-up table, more beautiful than ever. Alas, there were now lists detailing the make-up for each man, and a bossy supervisor calling out names in turn. One by one, the nobles and *chevaliers* went up. Then, to my relief, it was a free-for-all for us mere rankers in painted chain mail and soup-bowl helmets. Regardless of glares and growls I pushed forward to make sure of being in the right line.

After a short silence while she busied herself with affixing the sheet around my neck she said, 'Thank you for your note, but you need not have bothered.'

'Of course I must bother! I could not sleep for the worry of what you must have thought.'

The tips of her fingers were as cool as her voice. 'Well, we did wonder what had happened to you – !'

'I have explained in my note! These damned attacks I have had ever since I was wounded. The headache is so fierce that I can only lie down somewhere in the dark. If I could have come back, believe me that I would.'

'Don't *worry*,' she said. 'It was all right. There was so much happening anyway, what with Mr Olivier turning up and everything.'

'I came back as soon as I was able, but you had gone.'

'We left before the end.'

'We? Ah, Miss Joan and yourself?'

'A gang of us.'

While I registered this, she had finished. 'There,' she said. 'That's you done. And be careful now.'

Was that a mocking edge to her voice?

'Angeline, may we meet after shooting today?'

She hesitated. 'I am not sure that would be a good idea.'

'Then I shall sit here until you are sure.'

'Don't be silly. There are lots of others still to be done.'

I sat tight.

'You will hold up the filming. There'll be trouble.'

'That is too bad.'

'*Please!* People are beginning to look.'

I sat on.

'Tonight is impossible,' she hissed.

'Then tomorrow night.'

'All right. Now please go.'

The schedule this day comprised simple but endlessly repetitive shots of us lining up in stationary ranks, lowering lances or raising swords in the case of those who carried such weapons, and urging our steeds to make the first deliberate step forwards. These would be cut into the opening footage of the charge. All directors like to bank such shots to cover over any continuity gaps, and they always collect them before the big action shoot in case of injury to their players.

At the midday break a meal was brought to the site, everyone having the same food, whether director or humblest extra. Men sprawled everywhere on the grass, some eating, some smoking. All around me was the rumble of talk. Olivier sat not twenty metres away, his shaven nape bent as he listened to another figure whose identity I had now learned, the film cutter Reginald Beck who was acting as assistant director.

Dominic was some way off, with others who wore the fine armour of nobles or knights. He was not to be seen at such times with a mere trooper. Angeline I could recognize, over by the shooting brake. She was perched on a folding stool, her hair glinting in the sun as she turned to speak to one of the other girls.

In thirty hours we should have our tryst, providing that I was not then crippled or disgraced or on the run. Again I was seized by a schoolboy confusion of excitement and panic. I lit a pipe and puffed it hard and told myself not to be so silly. This whole business of the charge was becoming quite absurdly magnified. In the crazy way of film making it occupied as much attention as if it were a real battle looming. Even the peasant boys talked of little else. It was said that eminent guests would be coming to watch, just as in Napoleonic days the rich drove out in their carriages to picnic and observe the slaughter at Jena or Waterloo. Even reporters from the papers were expected. A photographer was making his way even now through the sprawling figures, Mr Bower by his side. They stopped while the photographer crouched to snap a group who squatted on their haunches, helmets off and smoking the little clay pipes as they gamed their pence away.

The photographer was using our German Rolleicord. Around his neck hung what was unmistakably an early Leica. Slung over his shoulder was the canvas satchel of his trade.

Something about the way he moved was strangely familiar . . . impulsive and disjointed like a colt who hasn't got used to his long legs. And his hair flopping over his eyes.

God in heaven! It couldn't be . . .

Instinctively, I turned away and pretended to be deeply immersed in the study of a small wild flower growing amid the grass near by. When I heard Bower's and Olivier's voices I raised a quick look. The young photographer was being introduced to Olivier. I took the chance and crammed on my silly helmet and got to my feet and stumbled away.

I spent the next two hours with my head bent, my face averted and my soup-dish tilted over my eyes as the photographer wove in and out of our ranks, click-clicking away. Would he never be satisfied?

I almost succeeded. Only wretched luck finally unmasked me. When the last shot of the day was declared acceptable, one particular gang of young Irishmen spurred their horses away with the whoopings of cowboys and Indians. Shoona reared in alarm and threw me.

So of course the nosey photographer came running. My helmet had been sent flying. I heard him gasp.

I fumbled inside my 'chain mail' for my spectacles, just to be sure.

104

'Friedrich!' he screamed.

'Hello, Martin, old chap,' I said. 'Actually it's Frederick these days.'

'And Ingrid Bergman,' cried Martin Kilner. 'Do you remember Ingrid Bergman?'

We were all three in the tent Dominic and I shared. We had a 'five-noggin' bottle, as it was called, of Powers's whiskey. The lamp was lit. Insects fluttered against the glass.

'How may I forget her?' I replied. 'I was so in love with her.'

'You cannot have been. *I* was in love with her.'

'Nonsense. You were too young.'

Martin turned to Dominic as if to make sure of including him in our reminiscences. 'We talk of the same Ingrid Bergman who is now a Hollywood star. You have seen *For Whom the Bell Tolls*?'

'I have better things to do than go to the cinema every day.'

To hell with his surliness. 'It was the summer of '38,' I said. 'I had just been promoted chief messenger and must spend my days cuffing idle and cheeky urchins of whom Martin Kilner was the idlest and cheekiest – '

'Not true!' he protested.

'What about the time you released a mouse in Zarah Leander's dressing room? I tell you, Dominic, he was a pain. Anyway, Ingrid once came and sat at the table in the cafeteria that I and some other fellows occupied. She was eating herring fillets, I remember. Ah, she was so fresh and lively and without airs. Afterwards, one of the others asked if I had noticed that she was pregnant. I did not even know that she was married! The husband turned up at the end of shooting to take her away, lucky fellow. She was supposed to come back next year to play a big dramatic part, that of Charlotte Corday who assassinated the revolutionary Marat in his bath. All the actors were offering to be Marat! Then Goebbels changed his mind. It was perhaps unwise to encourage thoughts of assassination. The film was cancelled and Miss Bergman went to make a movie in Hollywood instead.'

'*Escape to Happiness*,' said Martin.

I almost gave myself away by leaping to demand why America should have been any happier for her than Germany. Luckily, I checked myself, for it turned out that Martin was only quoting the English title of the film she made there.

'I think it was also called *Intermezzo*. With Leslie Howard.'

'Of course! A romantic story. How terrible about poor Howard being shot down.'

'You said the other night,' Dominic broke in sharply, 'that in time of war an actor was a soldier of his country and should be prepared to die for his country.'

'That is another way of looking at it,' I said. 'Anyway, the German public very soon found itself another little Swedish sweetheart to replace Miss Bergman. You remember Kristina Soderbaum, Martin?'

'I think so,' he said.

'Even Dominic would have been a fan of hers,' I said. 'In one film she was naked but for a fur wrap.'

'That would not be allowed,' said Dominic quickly. 'You're making it up.' Abruptly he rose to his feet and muttered something about having promised to meet some of the fellows in the bar tent.

As soon as we were alone, Martin's gaiety left him. For at least one minute neither of us said a word. When he did at last speak, it was in German, whose monosyllables made his questions all the blunter.

'What are you doing here?'

'We should stick to English, old chap. You know how even the Irish jump at hearing the German tongue. As for what I am doing here, I have already told you. I am earning the best wages since I came home, three pounds and ten shillings a week plus a further pound for my horse.'

'When was that again?'

'What?'

'When you came home, as you put it?'

'As I already said, my father came to Berlin in the crisis days of 1939. It was August, so hot in the studios the sweat ran down us as we argued, even hotter in my uncle's tenement. "I am nineteen," I shouted. "I should be free to choose." "Be free to choose what?" he shouted back. "War is coming and you will be forced to fight. In Ireland we shall stay out of the lunacy, God willing."'

I paused. I had to be careful. I gave him some more whiskey and tipped the rest into the enamel mug I was using. 'Water?'

'Please.'

I passed him the soldier's water bottle which Dominic insisted on our using although the water from it always tasted musty. It had been carried by his father in Spain, he said. What a night for remembering all our fathers . . .

'But how selfish of me,' I exclaimed. 'All this talk of my father and I have not asked you the latest news of Dr Julius and Frau Lottie. Have you heard from them lately?'

He hesitated. 'Directly, not for two years. By roundabout ways, we have had news that they were all right still last Christmas, and sent their love.'

'To Luise and yourself?'

'Yes.' It was only a whisper, or a sob.

'I am so sorry,' I said. 'I did not mean to upset you.' Clumsily, I put my arms around him and brushed with my lips the soft, floppy black hair I had once so loved to stroke.

He pushed me away.

'In their letters, while they continued to arrive, they wrote sometimes of you. How you called at their house, then the time my father bumped into you at Tobis. You were working on some picture about Ireland, he said – '

'Ah, *The Fox of Glenarvon*, or perhaps *My Life for Ireland*, which followed. What a sudden love for oppressed Irish! And what terrible films! Would you believe that – '

'How is that possible, Friedrich? That you were still in Berlin then?'

'If only you had let me finish, I was about to say how I dug my heels in and refused to leave with my poor father that time. Germany was my country now, I was sure. Who would choose to go back to a damp island with no films, no excitement? I even tried to join the Luftwaffe but my eyesight was too poor and in any case the filmworld was then still protected.'

He continued to look at me searchingly. I had to seize the initiative, I had to guess what awkward piece of hearsay he might fish up next.

'Would you believe it, there was actually a proposal that I should be seconded to the Promi to work for our beloved Reichsminister and producer-in-chief!'

He nodded. A bull's-eye.

'Your father told you of how it turned out?'

'No. No more than he had heard of the appointment.'

'Well, it would not have been for me, Martin, arse-licking in the Wilhelmstrasse. But I did not need to worry for too long. Heads were already being shaken because I was not more than half a German. The love affair with the Irish people was beginning to be over as quickly as it had flared up. When I received news that my father was seriously ill, God rest his soul, it was not too difficult to pull strings. Some Irish students were returning home via Spain. I came with them. It was too late, unfortunately. He had died at last of our German gas of twenty-five years before.'

'I am so sorry, Friedrich.' He was sincere. He seemed to accept my story at last, thank God. He relaxed and soon became animated again, his hands emphasizing all he said, his hair flopping, the light catching the front tooth that didn't quite align with the others.

He told me of the English family who had taken

him and Luise into their midst, and how at school he had felt so out of place among younger children, until he had cheekily talked his way into becoming a photographer on a local newspaper. From that he had gone on to become a photographer for a film journal and was now a photo-journalist for a picture magazine. He no longer lived with the English family but had a small apartment, or 'den' as he called it, not too far from the magazine offices. Luise was already eighteen and worked as a compto-meter operator in a hotel, also in London.

Then Dominic came slouching back. It was getting late.

Martin affixed metal clips to his trouser legs. The chemist in Enniskerry who had given him lodgings had lent him a bicycle, he explained, for an extra half-a-crown a week.

I reached for the paper book of *Henry V*. 'I have been reading the text of this play we film,' I said. 'Do you know it, Martin?'

'Only that it is supposed to inspire us all for the Second Front when it comes.'

I glanced at him. 'But here the French are the enemy.'

He laughed. 'We hope that people will not notice that.'

I flicked through the pages of the little book. 'The King has a fine speech on the eve of the battle, when his soldiers lie wondering what the next day will bring. You will smile, but I cannot help feeling something of the same on the eve of our battle.'

Dominic, needless to say, was deeply suspicious of

Martin. How did I know this fellow was what he claimed to be? He was the very type of refugee the English would use to detect flaws in the stories given by suspected spies, etcetera. I assured him I knew Martin Kilner well enough to see through any deception on his part. Alas, the morning was to bring fresh doubts.

I decided to attend the morning Mass. It must have been ten years since I last listened to the comforting gabbled Latin. My mother had been a devout person. My father, in my time with him, had sometimes hurried me into church for a few anxious prayers and to light a penny candle. As a Rhinelander by birth, my Berlin uncle was also a Catholic at heart, but the years he had spent in an artisan, and what had been for long years a strongly Communist, quarter of the city had robbed him of the habit of church-going.

Dominic dug me in the ribs, and motioned behind us. Silhouetted against the entrance was the long figure of Martin Kilner. As I watched, he lifted a camera to his eyes. Well, it was a natural shot for a photo-journalist.

But as we left at the end of Mass, we saw him again, in conversation with some others. Two of them wore macintoshes and hats. They were the secret policemen who had been shadowing Olivier at the Legion Hall dance.

'What did I tell you?' hissed Dominic.

'Doubtless, they are concerned with the security of any important visitors who may come to watch the charge,' I replied. 'They will obviously wish to check up on all strangers.'

At that moment the sound of laughter came from the group.

'That does not sound like a policeman asking to see a fellow's papers,' said Dominic. 'And who is that other man with them?'

I wished for the millionth time that my eyesight was sharper. He looked a harmless enough chap, about thirty-five years of age with a humorous, somewhat gnomish face, but appearances could be deceptive.

'Don't worry,' I said. 'I shall make it my business to find out.'

The opportunity did not occur until we horsemen were being accoutred. Martin, needless to say, was snapping away with his Leica. I made sure he took one of me, and steered the conversation towards the important spectators who were expected.

'The English ambassador is coming,' he said.

'Really? By the way, I thought I recognized the fellow you were talking to this morning – you know, with the two Irish Gestapo men.'

He laughed. 'Oh, that was Mr Betjeman. Such a comedian.'

'Mr Betjeman?'

'The press attaché at the embassy. He is looking after the ambassador's visit – '

I was no longer listening. Bulldog Drummond! The famous adversary of our Carl Petersen. That was a different kettle of fish altogether. What was Martin playing at?

At make-up I had to force myself to pay Angeline the attentions due her, but eventually had her smiling.

'See you after the battle,' I said as I rose from the chair. And she nodded. That was something to hold on to.

I have to say that we made an impressive pageant as we completed our final preparations and began to assemble at the head of the long incline. For the first time the entire small regiment of horsemen was in full fig. The horses were gowned in cloths of rich colours. Their masks gave even my placid Shoona a deathly look. When the nobles and knights dropped their vizors, red-faced Irishmen became sinister warriors, no more so than the fellow Fergus Simmons riding as the Constable of France. His mount was black, his armour was black, his helmet came to a cruel snout.

Down the range I could see two or three carriages and just pick out the hats and bright colours of women. My mouth was dry and my eyes ached from the light, which was not full sunshine but had a diffused glare to it.

To my chagrin, the camera car was now running smoothly.

There was much relaying of messages by means of a field telephone.

We were marshalled in our ranks, and then marshalled again five yards farther back.

We made two starts and were raggedly stopped again after a few paces. Once we got going properly there could be no calling back.

On the third attempt, at last, we changed from a walk into a lumbering trot. And then into a canter.

Nothing in the rehearsals had prepared me for what followed. Perhaps because the horses were blinkered by their elaborate face masks, my Shoona was hemmed in and jostled. The noise was indescribable. To the drum-roll of hooves was added the ringing of metal on metal and the clamour of voices. Caught up in crazed pretence, those around me shouted oaths, blasphemies and imprecations.

As we reached full gallop my chief concern was to hang on at all costs. Ahead I could see the Constable of France out in front, his sword raised high in his armoured fist. And yes, there to the left was the camera car. One small part of my mind even noted with admiration the slow pan that Hildyard, crouched behind the camera with Krasker, was executing. Then too many things were happening at once. The car was now slowing. In a moment we would start to overtake it. I had to be closer if I were to mask the shot. As I tried to pull Shoona towards the left we were buffeted and I cursed anew. She swerved and suddenly we were in the clear, hard up against the camera car but already speeding past it. There was no holding the stupid little horse. From somewhere a figure loomed up straight in front of us, oblivious to us. I tried to pull aside but there was a thump as we sent him spinning, and the next moment we were enveloped again in the mêlée.

When we pulled up at last, Shoona had gone lame.

I looked back. Ambulance men in blue uniform were hurrying to a spot by the track two hundred metres behind.

Seven

Angeline was waiting for me by the fine arched entrance to the estate which normally one did not use. She was chatting to the fellow with an armband who stood guard on the gate. My heart would have leaped to see her but for the fears that weighed it down.

'The poor fellow has been taken to the hospital in Bray,' the guard repeated for my benefit. 'They say it is his back that is broken.'

'Oh no!' I exclaimed. They looked so startled by the anguish in my voice that I hastily added, 'But people are saying that he should never have strayed so close to the charging horses.'

'Of course he should not,' said the guard, 'especially with his eyes pressed to his little camera so that he could not watch out for himself.'

'Did you see him, Frederick?' Angeline asked.

'Earlier in the charge, yes. I saw him when he was still quite in the distance and thought then that he was too close to our path. Later I was too hemmed in to see anything. No one, curiously, seems sure as to whose horse actually ran him down.'

'Perhaps he will be able to say who it was.'

This was what I feared, and which, together with remorse, hung over my best efforts to be debonair and carefree. For her part, Angeline seemed ill at ease. We walked to the town exchanging stilted remarks, nor too many of them.

'What are those large birds we see?'

'Someone said they are buzzards.'

'Buzzards?'

'A sort of eagle.'

And what was there to do when we arrived? There was nowhere in Enniskerry suitable for the entertainment of a young woman. In any case, the town was already filling up with filmsoldiers out to celebrate their battle.

In the main street I saw the bus to Bray about to leave, and on the spur of the moment hurried Angeline aboard. Then a strange idea came to me which again I put into operation before second thoughts could intervene.

'Before we do anything else,' I said, 'let us call and see how Martin is.'

'Martin?'

'The poor photographer.'

The small hospital was run by nuns, who seemed surprised by our arrival. There was much scurrying off to consult some superior authority before we were given a smile and told that the patient was drowsy after having his collar-bone set under anaesthetic –

'Collar-bone?' I interjected.

'That and a cracked rib and shock, of course,' said the sister.

'And not his back? The Good Lord be praised,' I cried.

– but that we might see him for a moment. I thanked her warmly, remembering that Goebbels always chose to be nursed by Catholic nuns rather than the grim sisters of the lay order set up by the Party.

Martin's face was almost as pale as the linen pillow on which his head rested. There was a bowl by his side. I allowed myself a revised, lesser pang of remorse, but he opened his eyes and managed a smile when he recognized me.

'This is Miss Angeline Byers of the make-up department,' I said.

And of course she was very feminine and sympathetic. As we made the small talk one makes on these occasions I knew that my instinct had been sound. It was soon clear that Martin had no idea who had ridden him down; far from being suspicious, he was touched by our visit. As for Angeline and me, we now conversed a little more freely, though still as strangers.

'How is it that you already knew each other?' she asked as we consumed a meal of fish and fried potatoes in the best hotel Bray could offer.

'Oh, Martin came to photograph Ned and me when we were brought back to England after our ship was hit. You remember the *Bismarck*, the German battleship? I was aboard the *Prince of Wales* when she was struck by a shell from the damned Jerries.'

'But you are Irish.'

'There are plenty of us in your forces. Anyway,

there we were, Ned Knight and myself, being brought ashore from the hospital ship – '

'Esmond Knight the actor?'

'Of course.'

'I worked on his make-up for *The Silver Fleet*. His face was messed up terribly.'

'Poor fellow, he lost his sight. I was discharged with nothing worse than thick spectacles and a foul headache every week or two.'

She looked at me reflectively. 'And that was the only time you had met before – Martin and you?'

I took a sip of tea before answering. It was necessary to be careful. 'No, no, we became almost friends for a while – you know, two foreigners thrown together in a big city.'

'How sweet.' There was an amused glint in her eye I hadn't seen before. Miss Angeline Byers was perhaps not altogether the serious young woman I had supposed. But she immediately changed tack. 'He's just had an operation, you know – Mr Knight. He's supposed to be able to see again with one eye. Did you know he was going to be in this picture?'

'In *Henry V*?'

She nodded.

'Which part will he play?'

'Oh, I forget. Wait a minute – is there someone called Llewellyn?'

'Fluellen!' I cried. 'The Welshman among the four humorous captains who come from each of the countries of Britain. *For look you, the mines is not according to the disciplines of war.*'

To declaim this properly I put on a lilting accent such as the Welsh employ. Angeline looked bewil-

118

dered for a moment, before dissolving in a peal of ringing laughter which had all heads turning in the room.

'It is in the text,' I protested.

She continued to laugh.

'And you, Miss Byers,' I declared, 'are as heartless as you are beautiful.' But it had broken the ice, that merriment.

Afterwards we went to the 'second house' at the cinema in Bray. The feature was some foolish English comedy in which a male actor played an old Irishwoman. I thought it insulting, but the Irish around us did not seem to mind. They even found occasion to laugh.

As I rose to leave at the end, Angeline sat fast. 'There are supposed to be some rushes tonight,' she said. 'We could stay and see them if you like.'

'Rushes?' For a moment the English term puzzled me.

'The shots which have just been processed and sent back from the labs.'

Great God, yes! 'If you like,' I replied.

When the audience had shuffled out, only a minute or two elapsed before people from the film unit began to file in. Some waved to Angeline; one or two gave me a curious glance. I recognized the various designers, the costume chief and Menassian, the Technicolor expert. Krasker and Hildyard were early arrivals. Finally, Olivier entered with Dallas Bower and Reginald Beck, and the lights dimmed again.

The sequences were those preparatory ones shot on the day that Martin and I came face to face. The first leader strip flickered on the screen, the marker board was held and clapped, and then there was a line of thin, grey, bleached horses and men –

'What is this?' I blurted out. 'What happened to the colour?'

'Sssh. I'll tell you in a sec.'

As soon as there was a pause between scenes, she whispered that with Technicolor the rushes were always so. Mr Olivier had been terribly downcast when the first batch arrived, but George Menassian had told him that they always looked like something Edison had just invented. These were fine, they would print up beautiful.

At the end Olivier and Krasker and Menassian exchanged a few remarks. Then, as everyone prepared to go, Olivier hung back. He donned a stormcoat and pulled a wide-brimmed hat down over his eyes. I had seen him wear neither garment before, and must have shown my curiosity. 'It is to try and give the fans the slip,' said Angeline.

Alas, the ruse did not have great success. The crowd of young women and girls waiting outside the cinema quickly thronged around the disguised figure with squeals of awe, some brandishing autograph albums. One daring beauty planted a kiss on his cheek. The hero put on a show of rueful charm and made pleasant remarks, but as he freed himself at last and climbed into the waiting car I saw an expression of irritation on his face.

As for Angeline and I, we had missed the last bus to Enniskerry. 'Never mind,' I said, 'we will take a carriage.' As we clip-clopped through the dusk I took her hand. It rested in mine a cool, smooth little being with a life of its own. At the door of her pension she let me kiss her once before running inside.

Only Dominic knew that it was I who had collided with Martin. I had told him, of course, that it was entirely deliberate, a snap decision when I saw the figure looming ahead. 'As Leni Riefenstahl always says – one must exploit accidents when they are offered. If he was spying on us, which I doubt, that will stop him.'

I went to visit Martin again, this time alone. It was necessary to know if, for instance, the police had been to interview him about his accident.

'Merely a routine visit from a bobby with such an accent I could hardly understand a word he said.'

'And the Bulldog Drummond?'

'Who? – Ah, Mr Betjeman, you mean. He sent me the figs you see there. Do you like figs? Please take all you wish, but they are not very ripe. Did I tell you he is also a poet?'

God above, had I run down my once-dearest friend for fear of a poet?

'Of course,' Martin added, 'there was a message in invisible ink on the back of his card. It asked me to contact him if I came across any suspicious fellow I recognized as another German.'

I pretended to busy myself with a pipe. 'Have you?' I asked between puffs.

'Only you!' My face must have been a study, for he laughed delightedly. 'Friedrich! You were always so easy to tease.'

I threw my matchbox at him and missed. 'If you

weren't in plaster I would tan your arse for you.'

That out of the way, he told me extraordinary things about the circumstances of this film which had reunited us. I would never have learned as much – I now realized – from the poor contacts I had so far made. Even Angeline's gossip was limited to the small-talk of the studios.

Far from being a project of the English Ministry of Information, as we had assumed at the Promi, *Henry V* was a private enterprise. Oh, the Ministry had approved the idea because of its obvious relevance to the landing of English troops on the shores of Fortress Europe, if and when that were attempted, and the fearful losses that would follow. But their practical support had been limited to attempting to secure the release of a few actors and specialists from the armed forces, and that to no great effect. They had quite failed, for example, to get the Shakespearean Ralph Richardson I had seen in *The Silver Fleet*.

'But they have Esmond Knight, do they not?'

'Poor Ned, his fighting days are over. Though now he has some sight again. I photographed him when he returned home from the operation, you know.'

So I had been closer to the truth than I knew!

'Even getting hold of the camera had to be done by striking a bargain with Korda and Coward and Pressburger and all the others who wait for it,' Martin was busy telling me.

'What do you mean? That there is only one camera for all the film-makers?'

'Only one Technicolor camera. It is the only one

in Europe! Yet the ministry will not rule as to who shall have it.'

The most surprising fact of all was that none of the cost of the movie was being borne by the ministry, as would certainly have been the case with any propaganda film in Germany. The producer had to find all the money.

'He is an Italian,' said Martin, 'Mr Filippo del Giudice. I have also photographed him. Can you believe it? Only three years ago he was locked up as an enemy alien. Now he risks every penny he can borrow on the masterpiece – he says – that shall win the war!'

At this time, of course, Italy was still an ally of the Reich, if less and less a full-blooded one. It was indeed a strange circumstance –

'And with every day lost to the weather he must be more anxious?'

'You bet.'

The greatest set-back was still to come. The message must have reached Olivier that evening. It was all round the camp by nightfall, even if the peasants would have barely understood it. The great charge had been in vain. A deep scratch ran through every metre of film that had been exposed.

'But how is such a thing possible?' Martin exclaimed when I bore the news to him.

'All too easily possible, either in the camera or in the developing process. And with Technicolor, I understand, there are three negatives, which can only multiply the risk three times.'

'They will be so disappointed. All that great spectacle for nothing.'

123

'They will do it again. Few films escape such setbacks,' I added philosophically. 'When Veit Harlan was making *The Great King*, the Battle of Torgau had to be fought three times.'

Martin looked puzzled. '*The Great King*? When did he make that? I don't remember it.'

'After you left, of course,' I said hurriedly. I had always to be so careful. *The Great King* was not made until 1941, when I was also supposed to have gone. 'The only tragedy,' I continued quickly, 'is that the Battle of Agincourt may have been fought again without its most dashing *chevalier*. My faithful war horse has gone lame and the vet says that she must not run again for some days.'

'What about my pictures? They will now be of the wrong charge.'

'But just the same.'

'Suppose the French win next time.'

'That is not possible. It is in the scenario how the battle shall turn out – ah, you are joking!' Even as I laughed appreciatively, the idea crystallized in my mind. 'But if you are at all worried, old chap, why not let me stand in for you? I shall have nothing else to do if my horse is still lame. I can handle a camera, you can be sure. Even a Leica. I will not be as good as you, of course, but I will have the correct focus and exposure and perhaps some luck.'

Naturally, he did not agree straightaway. A photographer is as jealous of his work as any other artist. Deliberately I did not press the matter. In due course he raised it again.

'If you could just cover for me when they shoot the charge again,' he said. 'Anything turning out differently, that's all.'

'Of course,' I promised.

'Take care of my cameras, won't you? Especially the Leica. It was one of the first. My father bought it. I was never allowed to touch it. But when I was sent to England I found it in my case.'

'I will guard it with my life. Now is there anything else you need to complete your portfolio?'

He hesitated. 'I was hoping to get some shots of Mr Olivier relaxing in his caravan, but he kept putting it off.'

'Then shall I try?'

He shook his head. 'That is something I must do myself.'

I agreed while privately resolving it should have priority. From out of the blue had fallen the perfect opportunity, at the perfect juncture of events, to close at last on my quarry.

As it grew dark each day, the flickering light of candle or small lantern could be seen through the window or, on fine nights, the open door of Olivier's caravan.

The next evening I waited until the light at the window had been visible for about half an hour and then climbed over a small fence to make my way towards the caravan, carrying Martin's camera satchel as a badge of office rather than with any intention of using its contents, to which I had added my Walther pistol. I paused to light my pipe, addressed some words of greeting to sheep grazing near the caravan and generally made my approach as noticeable as possible.

Olivier was writing at a small table hinged to the bulkhead of the caravan. The candle burned in a glass holder just above the table, throwing its yellow light on the handsome, chiselled features.

'What do you want?' he said without looking up. I can still hear the little words biting the air as if Shakespeare himself had furnished them.

'Five minutes of your time.'

'Who are you?'

'You know me by my habit,' I declared. If quoting from the text of the play had broken the ice with Angeline, perhaps it would do the same for Olivier. These were the words by which the French herald Mountjoy introduces himself to the King on the eve of battle.

The ploy succeeded. Olivier looked round at once.

'Oh yes,' he said, peering at me. 'You're the photographer fellow. I thought you were in hospital.'

'I have taken his place.'

'I see.'

'What he particularly asked me to secure, if possible, are some photographs of yourself, sir.'

'Not in this light.'

'No, that would hardly be possible,' I agreed. 'I would like to arrange a session when I might snap away at leisure without robbing you of your valuable time. In other words, when you are occupied in some domestic task here in your caravan, such as making a cup of tea or writing to Mrs Olivier.'

Instinctively he put his hand over the sheet of paper on the table, then made an impatient sound.

'I'm writing to her now, as it happens. This is generally the first chance I get, so you are out of luck there.'

'If it were to be raining in the daytime – '

'Hah!' he exclaimed. 'If it were *not* to be raining is the dream. We have lost fifteen days already.'

'And the charge must be shot all over again.'

'Ah, thank you for reminding me of that.'

'Believe me, sir,' I said with unaffected sincerity, 'no one is more deeply concerned for you. I have had some experience of the filmworld and all the slings and arrows it can hurl at one. But if it is any consolation, no masterpiece of the cinema has been without its set-backs.' I drew breath and added, 'The epic film *The Great King* has had to fight the battle of Torgau three times.'

'Young man,' said Oliver, 'I was going to throw you out without more ado. I'm still going to throw you out, but we shall have a drink first.'

He half-rose from his seat to reach for a bottle of whiskey, wincing as he did so.

'Your ankle?' I asked solicitously.

'My back. I wrenched it some time ago. It was getting better.' He poured two glasses of the spirit. 'Water? Soda? Move that script and sit down.'

There was a canvas stool on to which had been tossed a thick script of yellow foolscap pages laced together at one corner. I did as I was invited. Olivier handed me a glass.

'What film was that again, the one in trouble with its battles?'

'*The Great King. Der Grosse König.*'

His eyes focused sharply on me. 'What are you

trying to say?'

'Merely that it is a German film. Concerning Frederick the Great.'

'How do you come to be familiar with German films?'

'My misfortune was to be an Irish student stranded in Germany when the war broke out. We had exchanges between Ireland and Germany, you know, called Humboldt Scholarships. I was such a scholar. It was '41 before I reached home by round-about ways.'

'We only returned to England that year.'

I nodded. 'After Miss Leigh and yourself had played your famous rôles together as Lady Hamilton and Lord Nelson.'

'Mr Churchill's favourite film, I'm told.'

'And one of Dr Goebbels's.'

He gave something between a snort and a laugh.

I said, 'To pass the time and also earn some money to live more comfortably, I found work around the studios. There were two films made about Ireland during that time, both rather silly propaganda against the English. I was an adviser on one of them, and able to correct some of the more absurd mistakes. You also worked for Ufa, I think, at Neubabelsberg?'

'Neubabelsberg! What a name for film studios! Yes, I made a film there once. Only the English-language version, of course. It was a long time ago, I was very young.'

'You are still remembered.'

'Really?'

'Or certainly was so when I was there.' I leaned

forward, knowing that it was now or never if I were to impart my message. 'Mr Olivier, did you come across the notion of the filmworld then? *Filmwelt* in German, filmworld – as one word – in English. The filmworld was all the people who worked in Ufa and Tobis and the rest; the actors and singers, the directors, the designers, the scenarists, the composers, the cinematographers. But it was more than that. It was a league, a community apart, an order of brothers and sisters devoted only to one thing. The filmworld had its own ideals and its own goals. It looked beyond the narrow frontiers of politicians or nationalists to an international cinema that might bring the peoples of the earth together in peace and harmony.'

This was all a lie of which Goebbels himself would not have been ashamed, and, like Goebbels's best lies, with a small piece of truth embedded in it. The filmworld did exist as a kind of freemasonry, but one devoted to its members' own interests rather than to any lofty ideals. Goebbels sometimes vowed to root it out, sometimes tolerated it and sometimes even held himself to be its leader.

I continued before Olivier could interrupt. 'The filmworld began in the time you were there, under the Weimar Republic. That is why films such as yours were made in two or three languages. It survived the coming of the Nazis. It accommodated the outbreak of war and all the patriotic feelings which naturally arise in time of war. It is alive today, if of necessity keeping its head down – did you know, Mr Olivier, that a director can be threatened with death if he refuses to obey an order to make this or that film?'

'All very interesting,' said Olivier. 'But what on earth has it got to do with me?'

'You are making a brave film with this King Henry. But it portrays the French as the enemy, although the French have been your allies and will perhaps be your allies again.'

'You should have read on, young man,' he trumpeted. 'You would then have come across the French and the English united by love.'

'Historically, a political marriage,' I said. 'But let that go. Mr Olivier, I announced myself with the words of Mountjoy, the French herald who brings your King Henry the offer of a safe passage home in exchange for ransom, and thus the saving of many lives. Though he does not accept, Henry shows his respect of this messenger.'

'Yes, yes,' he said impatiently.

'Sir, I am the Mountjoy who approaches you on behalf of those brave citizens of the filmworld. They invite you to join an epic film they are planning which will bring all the great nations of Europe together in a common cause, the English, the French, the Germans. Is not that a noble undertaking to which you would rather lend your heroic magnetism?'

I had glossed over the fact that *Kolberg* also cast the French as the enemy, nor was Goebbels's phrase for Olivier's quality the one I would have chosen with more time to think; the words had a Teutonic ring which the actor might not have found flattering. Otherwise I was quite overwhelmed by the force of my case.

Olivier was looking puzzled. 'And what is this common cause that is supposed to unite us?'

'Against the barbarians, of course. Against the sub-humans who threaten all our European culture.'

Olivier rose again, reaching for his crutch. He was not especially tall and could just stand upright inside the caravan. He said rather quietly, 'When we came to your country we resolved never to raise the matter of Ireland's neutrality. We are guests in your country, grateful for the hospitality and help we are receiving and would not dream of questioning your decision to stay out of the bloody war. It is your own affair, and that applies whether we are talking to Mr de Valera or the little girls who hang around in the hope of seeing a film star. Let me just make one thing clear, though, for your especial benefit. When we have won the war, and not a moment sooner, we might begin to think about films for peace. In the meantime the sole aim is to defeat the enemy.'

'But who is the enemy?'

He stared at me. 'Are you mad? For your information I have just been playing a Russian in another film – '

'*Demi-Paradise?*'

'You are well informed. Yes, I played a Soviet engineer. And I may tell you' – he paused as if speaking a line – 'that I found him an admirable fellow. Good night to you.'

'You will at least think over what I have said? If you wish me to return, merely hang a towel from the window of this caravan.'

'*Good night.*'

As I gathered up the camera satchel he ostentatiously turned his back. For a moment I let my hand rest on the butt of the Walther. Then, instead, I scooped into the bag the yellow script which I had moved in order to sit down. It might now be useful.

At first light next day I approached the field again. No towel hung from its caravan windows. But as I watched, Olivier emerged in pyjamas, and made water a few metres away.

Eight

So: if Olivier was not willing to join us, he must be conscripted. Just as I was deciding on a plan, a foolish incident intervened.

My Shoona was recovering from her lameness, the veterinary surgeon said, and should have gentle exercise. We ambled to a waterfall some miles from the big house, where she grazed while I compared the camera script with the original text. It was a fine piece of work.

I identified the scene Dominic was meanwhile filming. He had been chosen to be one of the party of villainous French horsemen, he told me with sarcastic pride, who circled behind the battle to attack the English camp, kill the boy soldiers who had been left in charge and set fire to the tents.

When I arrived back in the horse lines, the peasants were full of what had happened. Apparently Olivier had wanted a shot of one rider galloping directly to camera as they rampaged through the encampment. They had tried the shot several times. Olivier had been dissatisfied. Finally the horsemen had ridden full tilt, failed to swerve aside and crashed into the camera. The poor horse had his flank ripped open, the men were saying, and Mr Olivier, who had been peering into the camera at the time, had reeled away with blood pouring from his mouth –

'Is he disfigured?' I demanded.

They stared at me blankly.

Luckily, I spotted Angeline packing away her make-up materials. She said the camera eyepiece had gone right through Olivier's upper lip and into his gum. Both had required stitches and the lip was swollen like a ripe plum, but he had seemed much more concerned about the injured horse and its rider.

'Every inch the officer and gentleman,' she added with that sudden pertness of hers.

'Who was the rider?' I said, already suspecting.

'Don't you know? It was that friend you were with at the dance.'

I found Dominic in the bar tent, which only opened when shooting was over for the day. He was at the centre of a gang of fellow horsemen, suddenly quite the hero. When he saw me approaching his expression changed instantly to one of sulky defiance, but I pretended no more than amusement. A pint of stout was thrust into my hand, Dominic's new-found popularity evidently extending even to the comrade who up till now had been ignored or mocked.

'Twenty-eight stitches,' said the bandy little ruffian of a jockey. 'Can you believe it? Twenty-eight stitches!'

'That seems a lot for a lip wound,' I said.

He stared at me. 'It wasn't his lip. It was his whole bloody flank.'

'Mr Olivier?' I could not believe it.

'No, the poor bloody horse.'

'The vet says he will be all right,' Dominic said, as if to excuse the celebratory mood. 'There is talk of compensation.'

'Fifteen pounds!' cried the jockey. 'Hold out for fifteen pounds. He'll never be the same horse again.'

'Meanwhile,' said Dominic, 'there is a suggestion that I should ride your little mare as soon as she is fit again.'

'Yourself not being such a thoroughgoing horse-man,' said the jockey, to a lot of boorish laughter and repetition of the phrase.

I bore it smilingly but soon pleaded a task to perform and left them all. When Dominic returned to our tent an hour or more later, unsteady of step and stupid of manner, I was waiting for him.

'Right,' I snapped. 'Now tell me exactly what you were playing at?'

'Nothing to do with you,' he started to bluster. 'And anyway, about time somebody did something towards this stupid operation – '

I hit him hard in the midriff. He collapsed with much gasping and retching, and eventually brought up the evil contents of his stomach. When he had finished I invited him to clear up the mess before we proceeded.

'Are you telling me,' I said at last, 'that you rode deliberately at Olivier?'

'You rode that photographer friend of yours down,' he snivelled.

'A snap decision,' I said, 'by someone who is empowered to take decisions. You are not. Now did you or didn't you do it deliberately?'

'What difference does it make?'

'The difference between hitting you once for stupidity or twice for disobedience.'

'God, you think you're so bloody on top, you Huns. Not going so well these days, though, is it? What with Africa and now Sicily and the bomber raids – '

I hit him again anyway. 'Now please answer my question.'

He looked at me with hatred. 'All right. Your precious Olivier ordered me to charge at the camera. We had tried the shot four or five times and each time he'd look through the view-finder and said it wasn't close enough. Finally he said, "Ride at the camera. Your horse will swerve aside at the last instant." But it didn't, and now my poor Tomas has twenty-eight stitches.'

This, I could tell, was the truth. 'What of the camera?' I asked.

'What about it?'

'Was it damaged?'

'I don't know. Shouldn't think so, or they'd be carrying on about it.'

How blind of me never to have thought of attacking the camera. Of course, I had not known until Martin told me that it was the only Technicolor camera in Britain. To have knocked that out would certainly have put paid to the movie. Even without such knowledge I should have seen the possibility of a decisive blow to Olivier's morale. Or was it that I suppressed the thought? Was I still too much a creature of the filmworld, brought up to respect the camera as the instrument of creation?

Well, it was too late now. It would be cossetted all the time.

I became aware of Dominic whining on about something. 'What do you say?' I snapped.

'I said, why don't you just kill the man and be done with it?'

I stared at him.

'With that bow and arrow you've got hidden away. You fancy yourself as an archer, don't you? An arrow through the windpipe would be rather poetic, eh?'

'Are you mad?' I cried.

Events began to move quickly now, unless it is only a habit of the memory to condense the busy spells in life and fill out with detail less active periods.

Olivier added a large plaster on his lip to his other wound badges. The charge was held for the second time, minus one French horse-soldier and with a substitute photographer. After the usual false starts and delays, all went well – indeed, better than the first time, everyone said. There was no point now in trying to sabotage the filming, though as it happened I almost succeeded unintentionally. I had left Martin's camera satchel on the ground to give myself more freedom of movement, and then forgotten it. It lay by the side of the camera track, about half-way back, where it might just have come into shot. Krasker spotted it as he took a last look around and screamed at me. By dint of covering the Olympic distance of 400 metres in little more than a minute, I managed to snatch it out of the way in time. I was soaked in sweat.

As I stopped to enter our tent after having a shower I heard a muffled cry. Dominic was gripped by a powerful arm round his chest, and silenced by a large hand over his mouth. Both belonged to the red-faced IRA man who had kidnapped me from the Legion Hall. The dark man with narrow features sat on one of the fruit boxes that served us both as seats and lockers. He nodded civilly.

The red-faced man released Dominic, and asked sarcastically, 'Was the water good and hot still?'

'Excellent, thank you.'

'Thanks be! I was mortally afraid it might all have been used by the others.'

'Not when they are Irishmen,' I said cordially, while glancing covertly at the camera satchel where I had dumped it earlier. Had they looked inside and found the Walther? Or the bow and its arrows concealed in my bed?

'Your friend tells us you performed a feat of running,' said the dark man sardonically.

I looked at Dominic, who held my gaze for a moment but then shifted away. 'Then he will also have told you why it was necessary,' I said. I gathered up the satchel and put it by my bed and continued to towel my wet hair. 'You have stupidly put me at risk by coming here.'

'We do have some experience of getting around our own country without attracting attention, Mr Harris. With everyone's eyes on the great run of the horses, not to mention the even greater run of yourself, it was not difficult. What you should be worrying over is why we have had to come, not how. Four weeks have passed and you have made no contact with us, as you promised. We are entitled to know what is going on.'

'What *has* been going on,' I snapped, 'is the quest I was ordered to pursue first – Olivier's voluntary co-operation.'

'And have you got that?'

'There is still a possibility. But I was about to plan the next course, which is to take him whether he wants to go or not. To kidnap him. The only problem is that there is no possibility of a U-boat rendezvous for another two weeks.' While I was speaking I sat casually on my bed. It seemed not to have been disarranged.

'A bird in the hand,' said Red-Face heavily, 'is worth any two in the bush. We can always knock him on the head to keep him quiet until it is time to wave him goodbye.'

'And by which same time there will be such a hue and cry that everyone will be on the look-out. Can you not imagine how the English will be laying down the law?' Absently, I reached for the satchel.

'Again, we do have some experience,' said the dark man mildly. 'We have our hideaways, our lines of communication.'

'Very well,' I said. I reached into the satchel and brought out Martin's small diary. The Walther was still there. 'Now listen. Do you know what is meant by "rushes"? They are rough prints of the scenes that have been filmed. Whenever a batch of these rushes arrives from the laboratories they are shown in the cinema at Bray. It is usually quite late in the evening, after the regular performance in the cinema. Olivier always goes. Afterwards he slips away wearing a hat and a raincoat with the collar turned up, in order to avoid the attentions of film fans.'

The dark man nodded.

'The next batch to arrive will be of the charge today. They will be at the labs some time tomorrow. At the earliest they will be on their way back the next day. They could be screened on Friday night. That would be the opportunity.'

The dark man said. 'The expenses as we agreed?'

'Of course.'

'In sovereigns?'

'Half in notes, half in sovereigns.'

The red-faced man lumbered over. He moved quickly for his bulk. 'In that case, let's be seeing the darlings.'

'When you have earned them is time enough.'

A huge hand hauled me to my feet. The red face was thrust close to mine. 'The gold,' he bellowed.

I hacked him expertly down the shin and, as his grip loosened, seized his right wrist and twisted his arm in a simple wrench. The unarmed-combat instructor at Friedenthal would have been rather pleased with me. The fellow was now half-turned away from me, of course, and bent forward. I scooped the Walther from the canvas satchel and applied the muzzle, not too gently, to his skull just behind the ear.

'Sit down quietly,' I ordered, 'or I shall be obliged to shoot you.'

'Do what he says,' commanded the dark man, his

expression unaltered. 'All right, Mr Harris,' he said to me. 'You have made your point. We accept your terms. In return, I must ask for your help in the operation.'

'Of course.'

'And that of your friend as well.'

'Why?' Dominic did not look eager.

'Because we shall pretend to be college students on a prank, as when they raise money for charity. That way, the subject will be less alarmed. We therefore need a few volunteers in the squad who look somewhat less that thirty-five years of age and' – he glanced at the red-faced fellow – 'less than eighteen stone in weight.'

'I want nothing to do with such ignorant thugs,' Dominic whined when they had gone.

'You will do as you are ordered,' I said firmly.

Word came, ahead of the rushes, that the second charge was fine. The notice was posted the same evening that many of us horsemen would be paid off at the end of the week. Only the star riders would be kept on for the close-quarters shots still to be obtained. Dominic's name was among these. Mine, needless to say, was not. Well, it all fitted. Once we had Olivier, I would have to vanish anyway. With two thirds of the company riding off at the same time, my departure would not stand out.

I went to tell Martin I would be departing. He also had some news.

'The specialist comes again on Friday, and if he is pleased I shall be allowed to leave next day.'

'Oh, that is wonderful. Now you will be able to

take all the shots yourself that I have done so badly.'

'I am sure they are perfect. But of course, yes, I will try to get something, perhaps Mr Olivier with his wounded lip. As long as it's only one or two days. I have been away too long already.'

'We can write to each other if you like.'

'Oh, *yes*.'

To say farewell to Angeline was harder. On the last evening, as soon as she was free, we walked to the Pepperpot Tower, a small landmark on the Powerscourt Estate. Many birds sang, the air was soft and warm. We held hands and talked of much, but when I tried to draw her to the mossy ground she resisted and said, 'Not now, not here.'

'Tomorrow I shall be gone.'

'But we can see each other again somewhere, can't we?'

'What is wrong with here and now?'

'I hardly know you.'

'In wartime that is no longer important.'

'That is for me to say.' She ran her fingers through my beard. 'I wonder what you are like without your barbed wire.'

'Come with me to my tent and you shall see. I will shave it off.'

She laughed and shook her head. 'Not even for that. But you will come to England again, perhaps? To look up old comrades who fought at your side aboard your battleship?' Still laughing, she kissed me quickly and said, 'I'll give you our address.'

That night I did in fact shave off my beard.

We were to meet at the saloon by the railway station

in Bray. The others were already there when Dominic and I arrived – the red-faced man and one other fellow, perhaps twenty years of age, with a lean, wolfish face and bad teeth. 'This is Daniel,' said Red-Face.

Daniel shook hands with us and said something in so thick an accent of the Dublin slums that I could not understand him at all.

'Is that all of you?' I said.

'Jesus, are you wanting a battalion to take one fella, and him walking with a stick?'

I frowned at him to keep his voice down, and said, 'The idea was that we should be students.'

'And isn't Daniel the very image of a young gentleman from Trinity College?'

'What about you?' I demanded. 'I suppose you are the professor!'

Unexpectedly, he laughed aloud and slapped me on the back. I judged that they had already had more than a few drinks. According to the old clock above the bar there was still an hour to go. I would have to make sure they had no more.

As soon as I dared, I said, 'We ought to go now, to make sure we see the audience leave after the regular performance. After that, the rushes may only last a few minutes.'

'Just one for the road?'

'Sorry.'

'We are supposed to be young fellows out enjoying theirselves.'

'No!'

The car was parked in the station yard, an old sedan with room for three in the rear seat. That much was all right. How well it might serve in a pursuit was another matter, if the wheeze and clatter of the engine were any indication. Red-Face settled himself behind the wheel and we drove, none too smoothly, down the main street of the town towards the corner where the cinema stood. Red-Face pulled into the kerb about fifty metres short, and switched off.

'We have these,' he said, producing scarves of flannel striped in bright colours. I wound mine round my head to mask as much of my face as possible. It was rough to the raw skin I had lately shaved.

'And this,' Red-Face added, rattling a collecting can. 'We are collecting for the Irish hospitals, all right? Now you two, Dominic and Daniel, you are to accost the subject and bring him to the car – '

'I told you. He will easily recognize me,' whined Dominic.

'That's what himself has ruled, so just do as you're ordered. Mr Harris will head off anyone who tries to follow, but be sure to get back to the car. We tell the fella we're taking him just a mile or two along the coast to Dunleary, where there's a dance. He's just to say hallo to the people there and have his picture taken for the papers, and then we'll take him back to Powerscourt. All right?'

'And when he finds out that is not what is happening?'

'You can handle him, I'm sure, Mr Harris, with that way you have of coming the strong man.'

The people were starting to leave, the first ones hurrying to catch a bus or train, perhaps, others following more slowly and for a short while quite filling the street. A few lingered outside the entrance and were presently joined by young girls in summer dresses who were congregating from all directions. Obviously word of the screening had spread. At this moment the film-unit station wagon swept up. Four, five, maybe six figures got out. It was difficult to see because the crowd closed in but I was sure I spotted Olivier.

'There he is,' I told the others.

If the wagon remained there, it was going to be awkward. Fortunately, the cinema doorman motioned its driver to park round the corner. What an excellent doorman!

The band of young ladies waited on. They were no threat.

But where were the police, or Gardai as they were termed in the Irish tongue which no one used? Perhaps they, like us, were lurking in the shadows.

I became aware of sweating palms and a tightness within, as when my turn approached to leap from the parachute tower at Friedenthal. I had never truly believed this *coup de main* would take place, but now it was imminent . . .

I guessed the others felt it too. No one spoke. The air was thick with tobacco smoke and the smell of potatoes the Irish give off. I wound down the window by my side.

Suddenly there was movement again among the waiting girls.

'Quickly,' I snapped.

Red-Face had the self-starter whirring. At last the motor spluttered into life. We rolled forward. The figure with storm-coat collar turned up, hat brim turned down, was already pushing clear of his waylayers. I could hear their cries until Dominic and Daniel took off, whooping and shouting. I opened my door and prepared to block the way of any rescuers who might approach. But none did. I heard the rush of feet close to hand, more whoops, the bang of doors. The captive was thrust into the back seat between me and Daniel, and next instant we were screeching away in low gear.

Outside the town Red-Face slowed down, for there were no signs of pursuit. The engine noise subsided. The voice from next to me could be heard. I listened numbly. It was not Olivier's.

It was much more the voice of the cinematographer Jack Hildyard.

'I'm sorry,' he was saying, 'I'd like to help if I can, but I'm not the chap you want. I pretend I'm Larry to draw the fans while he nips out through the back.'

I struck a match and peered at the profile by my side. There was a large plaster on the upper lip. With my free hand I ripped it loose.

The man gasped. It was Hildyard.

Red-Face was snarling. 'Is it the truth he's telling?'

'Sure it is,' I declaimed in music-hall Irish tones. 'And could anyone with eyes in his head have supposed otherwise for more than a blink of the eye? 'Tis a craven apology we owe you, sir. Paddy there, turn around! We'll have you back in Bray in no time at all, and maybe find the right Mr Olivier.'

But by the time Red-Face had stamped on the

brakes and sworn under his breath and needed four
or five lunges forward and in reverse before we
could drive back into the town, there was no sign of
the shooting brake.

'Never mind,' I cried. 'We will take you to
Powerscourt. That is the least we can do.'

'No, no,' Hildyard said hurriedly. 'Not on your
life. I mean, it's all right. This suits me fine.' He'd
already reached across and got the door open. As he
lumbered past me he said, 'Here you are. For the
hospitals.'

It was a ten-shilling note.

'So what do you propose next, Mr Harris?' The dark
man's eyes were like flints.

It was a little after midnight. We had met him, as
arranged, at a house on the Dalkey road, but
without our quarry.

'Bearing in mind,' he continued before I might
answer, 'that from now on they will be watching him
like hawks. The Special Branch will hardly have
fallen for our pretence of a student prank. They are
paid to be less trusting. Let me put my question in
another form: now that attempts at both persuasion
and capture have failed, what is the next option?'

I said, 'I have no need to tell you that.'

He nodded. 'But who will carry it out?'

'Jesus,' said my red-faced friend, 'anyone can kill
the fella, it's the least trouble of all. Give me a
Thompson gun and I'll be back for breakfast wid it
done.'

'And the whole of the police and the army with
you,' said the dark man expressionlessly.

It was my turn to put a question – 'You say you have a secure house where someone might be kept for a while?'

The dark man nodded again. 'We have.'

'Good. Then there is something you shall do for me. The photographer Martin Kilner whom I regrettably had to injure is to be released from the hospital in Bray in the morning. He should not be too alarmed if you are there to give him a lift wherever he wants to go. Bring him to your secure house and keep him there until you hear from me again. Try not to hurt him.'

No one spoke.

'And make sure you have all his papers, etcetera. I may need them.'

'You will do it yourself?' said the dark man.

'One way or some other,' I said. 'Yes, I will do it.'

Rain drumming on the canvas, the first for many nights, woke me. It was still dark, but better that I should be early than too late. I slipped from my bed and felt under the straw palliasse for the bow. The two arrows were tucked between palliasse and blankets where, I had hoped, I would not lie on them.

I pulled on my clothes and gathered up the camera satchel with all the essentials in it for a speedy departure, should that become imperative and also be possible. Dominic was still sleeping soundly as I crept out.

About 150 paces from Olivier's caravan as an archer would have reckoned it, or 120 metres as I thought of the distance, grew a patch of coarse grass and nettles, now about waist high. I approached slowly and settled down behind it.

It could be a long wait. Already I was soaked from the rain, and beginning also to feel cold. At least these miseries kept me from thinking too much of the desperate feat I had ordered upon myself.

Once, I fancied, I heard a sound from the caravan and braced myself, my heart thumping.

Another time, a small cow came so near that I could smell its breath, faintly sweet and warm.

At last the sky began to lighten to the east, which was on the right-hand side as I crouched, shivering, behind the clump. The rain had stopped.

It grew lighter. Birds sang. I felt the first intimations of the warmth of day. I looked all around. There was no sign yet of guards posted on or near the caravan.

Suddenly the door opened and Olivier emerged. He wore a dressing gown over his pyjamas and paused to hold out his arms and breathe deeply. The plaster showed pink and stiff on his lip.

He moved again, for a minute seeming to be heading straight for me. I fumbled for an arrow. Then evidently he discovered that his feet or his pyjama legs were getting wet, and turned away, picking his feet high. He stopped with his back angled to me at about forty-five degrees. I could see his fine profile against the sky.

Fumbling the notch of the arrow into the bow string, I pushed myself on stiff legs. He continued to gaze towards the sun. I could just hear the sound of his urine splashing into the wet grass. I entered into the bow and hauled back on the string.

149

Something was wrong. Something was very wrong. The arrow was already drawn back to its full extent and yet I could feel nothing of the deep strength of the bow. The string seemed to yield, soggily, within itself.

Olivier had finished and was heading back towards the caravan. As he reached the door I rose heedlessly to my full height, took aim and snatched the arrow on its way. It dropped short to land in the grass with so slight a sound that even if Olivier had not banged the door at that instant he would have been unlikely to hear anything.

'All right,' I swore. 'It shall be as befits a hero and a king. No more skulking. We shall meet man to man.'

I learned from some TV programme a thousand years later – Ned was in it, I seem to remember – that it was important to keep the string of a longbow dry. At Agincourt the English archers stowed their strings under their tunics until battle was imminent.

Nine

Dublin's so-called airport was little more than a grass field with a few hangars and a modest control tower. The departure lounge consisted of a hut furnished with wicker chairs and a counter where refreshments were available. I asked for a cup of coffee and examined the Irish newspapers carefully. There was still no reference to the farcical escapade in Bray. It began to look as if we had, if nothing else, avoided alerting the whole world to our intentions. But one could never be sure: officialdom had everywhere become skilled in controlling the news that was allowed to be given.

Other passengers began to assemble. I studied them surreptitiously to find one who might be used to 'draw the scent', as they had put it at Friedenthal. A man of about forty who seemed nervous about something, perhaps the thought of flying, fetched a cup of tea and a bread roll with butter and marmalade to a small table, but after only one mouthful lit a cigarette. He took only two or three puffs of that before resting it on the ashtray in order to rummage in his briefcase.

I strolled past him. 'Good Lord,' I exclaimed, 'fancy meeting you again!'

He looked up with a startled expression.

'On the clipper from the States, that interminable journey – we played cards and talked about everything under the sun.'

He shook his head uncomprehendingly.

'We had the world put to rights by the time we saw the Shannon below us, eh?'

'I think you have the wrong person,' he said. His accent was usefully Irish.

'If you're not O'Connell, then I'm a Dutchman,' I exclaimed.

'No, no. Mallory is the name, I'm afraid.'

'I do beg your pardon. Forgive me. I could have sworn you were he, but it was a long night and we drank a bottle or two.'

I passed on as he smiled nervously, then I bought an ounce of tobacco at the counter and asked where the public telephone might be found. The operator seemed reluctant to attempt a call to England, even after I had assured her that I had a small stack of shillings and sixpenny pieces ready. 'There is always a delay on trunk calls across the sea,' she said. 'It is necessary to have a number to call back.'

'Then call the number,' I snapped. 'Just try, is all I ask. At this time of day there should not be a long wait.'

Sure enough, the instrument rang just as I heard movement in the lounge next door. I had searched Martin's notebook for a suitable number to ring in London. It didn't matter very much what sort of place it should be, as long as someone should answer, but a hotel might be particularly suitable for my purpose. I had found the names of two in Martin's untidy hand, one with a Temple Bar number, the other with a Mayfair number. This latter I had chosen.

'Claridge's,' it now answered in a female voice.

'I have a message for Mr von Damitz,' I said with an Irish intonation. I saw no harm in borrowing my superior's name.

'Is the gentleman staying at the hotel?'

'Just take the message as usual,' I rasped. 'Tell him that Mallory called. I am at the airfield now and must go. The plane is about to leave. I will arrive in London this evening with the . . . samples. Is that clear?'

She started to expostulate politely.

I cut her off. 'I must go, they are signalling for me' – as in truth a uniformed official was doing. 'Make sure von Damitz is told; Mallory is on his way.'

I hurried to follow the other travellers on to the tarmac. Mallory, I noticed with satisfaction, was ahead of everyone, clutching his briefcase.

The aircraft surprised me. It was not the elderly biplane I had anticipated but a sleek all-metal monoplane with retractable undercarriage; an American Douglas as I had seen in several films including, I think, *Lost Horizon*. The interior was more spacious and better fitted, I had to admit, than that of the most modern German airliner, the Ju 90. The windows, unfortunately, had been painted over so that it was impossible to see through them, which made the flight rather claustrophobic.

After we had been served quite a fine breakfast I went into the toilet compartment for a final check of my appearance. Martin seemed to have no passport, only an 'identity card' together with a 'travel permit' bearing a photograph. After some experiments I had decided against trying to substitute my own photograph on the travel permit. We were sufficiently alike to make the risk of being challenged on this score rather less than that of tampering with the permit; once in England I could also use a forged identity card with my own name which I had brought from Friedenthal.

Meanwhile I held the travel permit so that Martin's photograph was reflected in the mirror above the wash basin. We had been given this tip at Friedenthal. The human face is rarely symmetrical, and if you wish to match your face in the mirror with a face in a photograph, it is important to see them as from the same viewpoint. I had to part my hair higher than usual and also make it seem curlier, neither task helped by the haircut I had received as a French horseman. With some of the expertise I had picked up from watching Angeline at work, I darkened the hollows of my cheeks, and under the eyes. I made a handsome Jew, I could not help thinking. Unfortunately Martin did not wear glasses, so I had to make the journey blind as a bat. I had also left behind my trusty Walther for fear of a customs search.

The engine note had changed and my ears were popping as the plane descended. My mouth was dry. I sucked avidly on the barley sugar proffered by the steward. Up till this moment the planning and execution of the flight had occupied me. Now I suddenly faced the prospect, in a very few minutes' time, of coming face to face with the enemy in his own heartland. It was beyond belief! Only a few weeks earlier I had met at the Promi a Luftwaffe flier who had talked of taking part in raids on Liverpool. Here I was arriving at the same city as a passenger, if you please.

I tried to tell myself that from Ireland to England was but a small extra step, and that even if I were arrested it could only be a short time before the realignment of the world's great powers took place, as so long foreseen by Dr Goebbels, and I would be on the same side as my captors. I did not succeed. I must even have sighed aloud, for the passenger in the seat across the aisle asked if I were all right.

'I feel a little sick, that is all,' I said.

'We shall have landed shortly and then you will be as right as rain.'

She was a handsome woman of perhaps forty-two years, expensively dressed and with a voice I knew to be rather aristocratic. It occurred to me that I might usefully cultivate her acquaintance for the next minutes. I babbled on about normally being a seasoned traveller but had lately suffered an ear infection which had left me with my sense of balance impaired.

'Don't worry,' she said gaily. 'My husband is often like that.' She pronounced 'often' as 'orfen'.

'I am sorry,' I said sincerely.

'Oh, it's nothing to worry about. Hardly surprising, the amount of gin he puts back.'

I was rather shocked to hear this but continued to

make conversation as the plane's wheels squeaked on the runway and we presently rolled to a stop. As we descended the steps from the plane, I stumbled and nearly fell.

'Take my arm,' said my new friend. 'Better still, I will take yours.' In which fashion we walked across the windy tarmac to enter the building where my fate would be determined.

Inside were several tables behind each of which sat an official. In front was another chair to be occupied by every passenger he scrutinized. It was clear that here no mere formality was observed. The only sound was the low exchange of murmurs, until my companion said loudly, 'We might as well make ourselves comfortable if they will keep us waiting,' and led the way to a bench at the side of the hall. She produced a tortoise-shell cigarette case and offered me a cigarette with one end tipped in cork.

'I will smoke my pipe if you have no objection.'

While I lit it I did my best to take in the scene. Behind the functionaries at their desks were other watchers, some in army uniform. The nervous Mr Mallory stood in line two places ahead of the station we had vacated. At this moment a curious and particularly damned English thing happened. The people farther back in the line looked our way as if to invite us to reclaim our place in the queue.

'Come on,' said my lady friend. She took my arm again.

For my part, I babbled whatever nonsense I could drum up to sustain the impression that we were mother and son – no, that would not hold since our names and likenesses were so different. As woman

156

and gigolo, then?

'Next!' said a voice.

I drew a deep breath and sat down.

'Good morning,' he said pleasantly. I could distinguish only a blurred face, thick hair brushed back, a hand held out for my papers.

I gave him the travel permit, and had to imagine rather than see for myself the eyes flicking from photograph to me and back to photograph. He said, 'You have been professionally occupied in Ireland, Mr Kilner?'

'Taking photographs, yes.'

'For three weeks?'

'I was injured in an accident. A horse ran me down. In any case, the film I was photographing is still not finished. I may yet have to return.'

He made no reply to this but began to leaf through a large file of papers on the table.

From the next table but one came, at last, a small commotion. Mallory's voice rose in feeble protest as he was led by his interrogator towards the door of an inner office, a uniformed man falling in behind him. I watched as the door opened and the party disappeared inside. Now, surely, my man would want to share in the excitement and would send me on my way. But he appeared to take no notice. He returned to a paper in the file on which he had already paused, and looked up at me briefly once more.

'Would you excuse me a moment while I make an inquiry?' He was already scraping his chair back. He walked, head bent, like a university professor, towards a partitioned-off cubicle from which I had heard the sound of telephones.

At this moment, the door of the inner office opened and another official emerged to intercept my man. They had a murmured exchange. I saw the other official look in my direction. Then they exchanged the folders they were carrying, my interrogator disappeared into the inner office and this other one approached me.

'My colleague has been called away to help with another matter,' he said. 'Please excuse me while I make myself familiar with your circumstances.' He turned over a page in the file.

I glanced about me. My new friend had been cleared and stood waiting while someone else took her place. I became aware of my heart beating, but otherwise continued to feel strangely calm, as if everything were out of my hands now, as indeed it was.

'I don't think we need detain you any longer,' said the official. He took a rubber stamp, inked it carefully on an ink pad, stamped my travel permit and handed it back to me. 'Good day, Mr Kilner.'

A curious dark-blue bus took us from the airport to the town centre. At the front it was a single-decker, at the rear it appeared to become a double-decker. In fact the seats were raised here above a hold for the passengers' luggage. My new companion sat by my side, puffing on another cigarette. 'I'd have the car to meet me,' she said, 'but petrol's so tight now, and anyway, George says we have to set an example.'

'The King?' I asked.

'Good God, no. George my husband.'

Now that I had retrieved my regular glasses I

could see her clearly. Though quite old enough to be my poor mother, she had a fresh complexion, large blue eyes and an amused look to her. She wore tweeds of quality, and a fine string of pearls. I caught a whiff of perfume of the headiness I had not smelled since I left Berlin.

Naturally I was avid to take in my first impressions of wartime England, but the bus windows were almost as thoroughly obscured by adhesive tape as the plane's had been. Through the narrow slot that remained I saw familiar suburban streets of little houses, each with its tiny garden. Tramcars running along a segregated track between the two carriageways of the road I did not remember from my childhood, though of course something of the sort could be found on the outskirts of many German cities.

Presently we began to approach the city centre, with tall buildings pressing in, and glimpses between them of cranes and warehouses and the funnels and masts of ships. I was gratified to see that many of the gaps were not there by design but by the efforts of our bombing planes. Sometimes half a street had gone, leaving only a littered open space in which weeds and wild flowers grew. There were buildings shored up by heavy timbers, and others standing only as roofless shells.

'That was Blackler's,' said my friend. 'Rather a good store, for Liverpool. They've got some little shops in Bold Street now, but it's not the same. D'you know Liverpool at all?'

'Not really.'

'Had a lot of life when the transatlantic liners used

to dock here. Well and truly passé by the time the war came. Lewis's went the same night as Blackler's, a couple of years ago. I happen to know because I was here. I used to drive an admiral about. Are you going to London?'

'Of course.'

'Your next decent train is two o'clock. We might have lunch, if you like.'

'Only providing I may be the host.'

'Fiddlesticks! We're birds of passage together, that's all. What's your name?'

'Frederick Harris, at your service!' There was no reason to suppose she had overheard the name of Martin Kilner under which I had been travelling so far, and it might be useful to be known by some persons under an alternative identity. I allowed a little Irish brogue to attach to my speech.

'I'm Jane MacMorris,' she said.

I pondered that name while we took a breath of air, as she put it. We deposited our luggage at the station and strolled down to a kind of plaza by the River Mersey. There was certainly a plentiful breath of air to be had from a strong breeze blowing off the river, which at this point, close to the sea, must have been at least a kilometre across. Ships of every kind moved up and down and across the turbid brown water, the sound of their sirens cutting through the constant cries of the seagulls which swooped everywhere. I was reminded of Hamburg or Danzig.

Some splendid imperial buildings were grouped on the waterfront, though at ground level their windows and entrances were obscured by sandbag revetments which in many cases were now leaking and discoloured. Shop windows were either boarded up, leaving only small portholes through which the passer-by might see the goods on display, or criss-crossed by tape. Well, Berlin was fast becoming the same. Looking up, one saw fat barrage balloons shining in the sunlight as far as the eye could see. These were many times more numerous than around such German cities as I had seen.

Green trams clattered along the street. There were also buses, some cars and vans and military vehicles. I studied with interest the people who thronged the pavements. Except that few of them now bothered to carry the gas masks in square cardboard boxes familiar from the English newsreels I had sat through at the Promi, they were much as I had feared; that is, pallid and shabby but, despite our great efforts in the sea war, apparently not actually starving.

We passed a 'cafeteria' in which people were lining up to be served with food of some description. Another time one could look down into a bar below street level in which better-dressed men were sitting at a marble counter eating shellfish. Our own repast was taken amid the faded pink and white and gold of a hotel which, Jane explained, was a relic of the great old transatlantic days. In such places, of course, the rich would always be able to command what they willed. Imagine my surprise, then, when Jane made some remark about a five-shilling limit on restaurant meals. A quick glance at the menu confirmed this fact. About one dollar in the currency rates of the day, or two Reichsmarks fifty, it would scarcely have bought a herring fillet at Horcher's! Yet we had soup, fish and a pudding made of carrots and dried fruit, with custard. The only extras I was allowed to buy were a bottle of the Irish stout for which I had acquired a liking, and two or three large gins for Madam.

'At a pinch one could get by without a ration book at all,' she said.

'I may have to,' I said, for I had become aware as we talked of this omission from my hasty plan to come to the enemy's heartland.

'They should have given you a visitor's card when you came through immigration. Uncle Fitz gets one every time he comes over.'

She had come from, or had married into, a so-called Anglo-Irish family, with property both in the Free State and in England. Her husband, this George of whom she had spoken so disrespectfully, was in the army.

Their children were at boarding school or, in the case of the eldest, at Cambridge University before joining the army. I tried without success to judge just where her loyalties lay.

'Mrs MacMorris,' I mused –

'It is Lady MacMorris, actually, and you must catch your train.' She began to gather her things together.

'Works to be done, and nothing is done, so help me God,' I quoted in a thick Irish accent.

She frowned. 'Now what is that from?'

'It is said by Captain MacMorris, the Irish captain, in the play *Henry V* of Shakespeare. Your family is perhaps descended from him.'

'I don't know about that,' she said, but giving me

a reflective look through her cigarette smoke.

'Perhaps I may telephone you when my duties are done.'

She rummaged in her handbag for a card. I took it as I had seen gentlemen do on the movies, without looking at it. We shared a taxi the short distance to the station to recover our luggage. She had to go to another station, she explained, for a local train to her home. When she held out her hand in farewell, I kissed it. She smiled. It was with some confusion of feelings that I settled into a first-class compartment and opened the *Henry V* shooting script in order to bring myself back to the task on which I had come.

After waiting my turn in another English line I took a taxi from Euston Station the quite short distance, as it turned out, to the address on Martin's papers. Or rather, I gave a street number two or four from the right numbers so that I might study the lie of the land before trying his keys. It was still full daylight and I did not wish to pinpoint my arrival.

The street was of nondescript buildings not more than four storeys high. Some had shops at ground level, one a small café still open. Others had a number of bell pushes by the door and names written on cards. I pretended to be searching among those next door – each had only a single woman's name, such as Trixie or Michelle – while peeping sideways. Number 34A, I saw, was the basement, reached by its own dingy flight of stone steps. Without further hesitation I descended to let myself in.

As I opened the door there was a fearful squawking noise and something rushed past me into the dark recesses of the sunken area. It was only a cat, naturally, but gave me an absurd fright. Inside, there was an empty saucer on the floor on which I trod. The air stank as in a ghetto. Master Kilner evidently did not share his parents' fondness for luxury. But after I had forced open a window on to the area and made a tour of inspection, I began to feel that I had a safe refuge for the time being.

I stood in silence for a while to detect any sound of immediate neighbours. There was none. The street outside was rather quiet, though sounds of traffic came from not far away. There was a small kitchen, a lavatory with wash basin, a windowless closet which Kilner had converted to a darkroom, and one large room which served both as bedroom and living quarters. In a cupboard I found some tins of food, jars of various things, a tin containing biscuits, a solitary egg, the stale end of a loaf. I had just set a kettle on the gas-ring when there came the sound of a key in the door.

Instinctively I slipped into the lavatory, realizing too late that I had left my baggage in full view of the entrance.

'Pussy, pussy, pussy,' came a rather clear little voice. 'Where the hell are you? Pussy, pussy, pussy! Want some dinner?' Then a brief silence and a cry in a different tone of voice altogether, *'You're back! Martin!'*

I emerged from the lavatory to have arms flung round my neck and as quickly unfurled. She gave a small shriek.

'Luise!' I said warmly. 'Martin is still in hospital

in the Irish Free State. You remember me? – his friend Friedrich?'

She stared at me without saying anything. She had grown up pretty and plump, with dark hair falling on each side of a smooth face with prominent eyes and a small mouth. She wore a dark-blue skirt and jacket with a blouse underneath.

'I was about to make a cup of coffee,' I said. 'Would you care for one?'

In the event, Luise took over the process, mixing some powder-milk with cold water to make white coffee for herself. She listened attentively as I chatted, except when the cat signalled its return by scratching at the door and mewing and she leaped up to admit it and put down a saucer of food.

'That is one thing about working in a hotel,' she called over her shoulder. 'Always plenty of scraps for the animals. Oh, but I'm being thoughtless. You must be starving after your journey.' She immediately began rummaging in the cupboard. I could not help noticing the shapeliness of her legs, accentuated by the fine seams of her stockings.

'Please let me take you to a restaurant,' I said gallantly.

'No, no. You must also be tired. And I should be getting home.'

'Martin particularly asked me to look after you.'

She peered at a little watch suspended upside-down from a brooch on her breast. 'I could give them a ring at home, I suppose, to tell them I will be late.' We walked a short distance to where the streets were more thronged, though no grander. My companion said this was the quarter known as Soho.

165

Many soldiers and sailors and airmen walked along rather aimlessly, calling and whistling to any women in sight. It gave me a curious sensation to be brushing so close to the uniforms of the enemy – or rather, the enemies in the plural. There were badges indicating such nations as Poland and Canada, also pretenders to be 'Free French' and, of course, many Americans. I was most interested by these visitors from another world. Their uniforms were incomparably superior to the coarse serge of the English rankers, the smoke of their cigars and cigarettes hung fragrantly in the air. But their military bearing was not impressive. One of them gave Luise a long wolf whistle, as I learned to call it, accompanied by an insolent stare. I was all for handing him a punch but Luise seemed used to it.

She led me to a small restaurant, again below street level, which was crowded with noisier and more excitable people than one expected to find in England. They were artists, actors, dancers, etcetera, I was told. The food was said to be Eastern, that is, greasy meat served on skewers. I demanded some wine and after handing over the money in advance, took delivery of a bottle brought to me by a swarthy errand boy. This was all an elaborate device, Luise explained, to get around the laws which controlled the sale of alcohol.

She wanted to know everything I could remember of Martin, plus all I could invent. Stories of the filming intrigued her, particularly when they concerned Laurence Olivier. As one knew from the 'fan' magazines, he was the object of much romantic adulation. 'What's he really like?' she asked. 'In *Fire*

Over England he cried, you know. Some people thought that very soppy, boys especially. But he was ever so good in *Lady Hamilton*.'

'He has heroic magnetism,' I said.

By the time we returned to the basement abode it was beginning to get dark. I switched on the electric light.

'The blackout!' screamed Luise. 'The warden's a fiend around here.'

She made me turn the light off again while we drew thick black curtains across one window and pushed and pulled a wooden frame covered with black paper into another. She kicked off her shoes and climbed on to the sofa to do this. I could not help being aware of a rounded seat nudging against my arm, nor of smooth legs and exquisite small feet with painted toenails –

'Your toes!' I blurted out. 'But I thought you were wearing silk stockings.'

'Out of a bottle,' she said. 'I've only one decent pair left and I'm keeping them for my sister's wedding next month – I call her my sister, she's actually our guardian's daughter.'

'Then please permit me . . . ' I switched on the light again to rummage in my case, and produced one of two pairs I had brought from France.

'Ooooh.' She turned the pack over in her hands. When she looked up her eyes were wide. 'Real silk!'

'Of course. Try them on.'

'Not now.' She looked at the packet again. 'The size is in French.'

'They will be right for you. But try them.'

'No, no. *These* I will keep for the wedding. They

167

are like gossamer. Oh, you shouldn't have.' She reached up on tip-toe and kissed me on the cheek.

I closed my arms about her and felt her go tense. She tried to push herself free.

'Please, don't be silly.'

'Silly?'

'You know what I mean. I hardly know you.'

'But those times I came to your parents' apartment. I watched you growing more beautiful each day and fell a little more in love with you.'

She laughed. 'Since I was only twelve, I don't think that can be so.'

'Do you remember your birthday party? I brought you a little book of blank pages, pink and green and yellow, and when I saw the other lovely things you had been given I was so ashamed – '

'But it was lovely. I have it still.'

'In any case, your mother held it up and said what a beautiful idea, and that she would be the first to paint a picture in it. Then everyone was calling out to ask if they could be the next.'

I became aware that Luise's eyes had filled with tears.

'Forgive me,' I said tenderly. 'I should not have reminded you of those days.' I enfolded her again in my arms, and this time she did not seem to object. I kissed her brow and was instantly in the grip of the passion a soldier feels as he embraces a maiden after months at the front. My mouth sought hers, my hands pawed at her plump Jewish body. She immediately began to struggle and cry out again. My hold tightened and I pulled her towards the sofa. Suddenly, there was thunderous banging on the outside door, and a voice shouting something I could not make out.

Immediately I switched off the electric light again and turned the latch. Outside it was almost dark now. A faint ray of light from a torch masked with paper was shone into my eyes, behind it an angry face surmounted by a flat steel helmet as worn by the Tommies.

'Very sorry,' I said. 'The blind was not fitted.'

'I've told you before,' the face roared. 'I shan't warn you again.'

As I renewed my apologies, Luise thrust past me, clutching her bag in one hand, her shoes in the other.

'Just a minute,' she cried to the warden as she wobbled on one leg to pull a shoe on.

'Bloody aliens,' said the angry face. 'They're the worst.'

'Sorry I have to go,' she called, preceding him up the stone steps. I slammed the door to and fixed the frame as best as I could in the dark. Wretched little temptress! But she had saved me from racial defilement.

By morning I was cursing myself. I had hoped to have three or four safe days in Martin's den before his disappearance might be noticed. Now I had to move on immediately: there was no knowing to whom Luise might prattle.

I stayed at small hotels near the railway stations, and once in a better hotel of which I had heard, where for only five shillings one could have a bed made up on top of the bath in a small bathroom. I befriended a merchant sailor who had drunk too much, stole his identity card and lodged two nights in a comfortable club that was run for seamen.

I walked through the streets and squares of the city, observing what I observed and taking the occasional photographs. We had been warned at Friedenthal against trying to buy maps, but in a bookshop piled with ancient musty volumes I found a booklet map of London and the Environs which was not too old and whose purchase, I judged, would not arouse suspicion.

I located on it the film studios at Denham where *Henry V* would resume shooting, and not far away from there the outer suburb of Rickmansworth, the home-quarter of Angeline.

On the eve of the 'August Bank Holiday' when an extra day's holiday was added to the weekend, I travelled there on the Metropolitan Railway, a journey of perhaps half an hour, and found a small hotel run by a friendly couple. With fluttering heart I sought a telephone box, and asked for the number Angeline had given me.

Ten

The water was brown as amber when one opened one's eyes after diving from the diving raft and rose towards the surface. On the lips it tasted of dead leaves. The sun was instantly hot on the skin as we hauled ourselves back on to the raft.

'Race you back,' called Angeline. She poised herself a moment on the one-metre board, and I marvelled again at the Aryan perfection of her form. Her legs were long and straight, her hips slim, her back golden in the sunlight. With her hair crammed into her green bathing helmet, her fine neck was revealed.

A thrust from the legs launched her into a passable dive, only a little flat. I followed with a racing dive, deliberately flat, and a lazy crawl so that I might remain a yard or two behind until she reached the shallows, when with two or three strokes I caught her up and we splashed ashore together.

'You beast!' she cried.

'No. An exact tie. Congratulations!'

When I met Angeline she had straightaway proposed that we should spend the afternoon at the

'Aquadrome'. I imagined some ultra-modern swimming pool of concrete and steel; it seemed to be, in fact, a natural lake set amid trees. One paid to gain admission, and some attempt had been made to provide agreeable recreation – the diving raft, a café, a beach for children; somewhat like the Wannsee in Berlin, if on a smaller scale and of less refinement. Certainly, it was well thronged. The grassy surround was strewn with sunbathers, music from a portable gramophone not far from us mixed with the shouts and laughter of those in the water.

'Ah, this is heavenly,' sighed Angeline. She lay stretched out on a rug. Her fair hair, released from the bathing cap, spread like a fan behind her head. The fine hairs on her limbs glinted in the sunlight. Though she had tilted her sun hat over her eyes against the glare, she was perhaps conscious of my intense gaze, for with the automatic, delightful habit of young women in bathing suits her hand checked the straps and edges to make sure no small arc of breast or buttock had crept into view.

'I will fetch some tea,' I said abruptly, reaching for my leather purse – Angeline had laughed at a man having a purse, but it is useful enough when all one is wearing is a bathing trunk, and that not one's own. Angeline's mother had found me one of her husband's when I explained that I had no costume with me in England. It was rather large for me, with a kind of overskirt to mask my anatomy: not the most flattering of garments.

As I made my way towards the café, laughter and raised voices came from the row of changing huts. A number of officers in air-force blue and some girls in

– or partly in – uniform of the same colour had evidently just been dressing after their swim. They were still tying their ties and combing their hair. One of the officers called out and at the same time tugged at the door of a hut. It opened to reveal two or three more young women virtually unclothed, who screamed and giggled as they covered themselves.

This also was unsettling, especially as I noticed from their badges that the officers were Polish, an inferior race. I obtained a 'tea tray', which included two small buttered muffins, and carried it back. As I approached our spot I observed that Angeline was talking to someone who stood over her. Without my glasses I could not see him clearly, but could at least tell that he had a head of dark curly hair and that his body, naked above the waist, was either dark skinned or much tanned by the sun. He wore only cotton trousers, with a towel round his neck.

Alone in an enemy land, one shrinks from all meetings, and instinctively I slowed my steps. But at this moment the stranger made a gesture of farewell and went on his way.

'Who was that?' I demanded as I set down the tray.

'No one in particular. He knows about horses.'

'I did not know you were interested in horses.'

'I had my own pony in Allahabad.' She busied herself pouring the tea, before continuing sharply, 'Is there something the matter?'

I pulled myself together. 'Good heavens, no!' Indeed, what more could a fellow ask than sunshine, sport and the company of a fine young woman? It was simply that Angeline seemed cool to me again, as cool as on our first meetings. Perhaps it was being back on her own territory, among her acquaintances.

I encouraged her to talk about the last days of the film unit in Ireland and the gossip of the studios on their return, partly to help her regain her ease with me but principally to learn all I could of the next scenes to be shot. She produced a version of the attempted kidnap at Bray in which it had already become one of those elaborate anecdotes, quite divorced from reality, which are passed around the filmworld. Well, that was perhaps no bad thing.

Her chief news astounded me. Though Martin had told me about the Italian de Giudice raising the entire budget for *Henry V*, I could not believe what Angeline now said, that he had been all but bankrupted by the prolonged Irish filming and had been forced to sell out to a rival.

'And the Information Ministry would not provide support?' I had asked. 'What if the film had been abandoned?'

She shrugged.

Of course, Dr Goebbels was all for making Ufa and Tobis finance their own films whenever possible. He could play tough, too. But if one of his favourites projects were to seem in danger, he would swiftly issue orders for its completion, and the production chiefs knew that the money would be forthcoming. There was quite a science in contriving such matters.

Angeline was searching for something in the cotton hold-all in which she had brought the bathing things. I guessed it might be a cigarette, and produced a packet I had been able to buy in London. She took one and lit it and lay back in the sun again.

'When exactly does shooting start again?' I asked casually.

'Next week. The ninth.'

'On the sound stage?'

'Outside, if the weather's fine. They've got to get all the close-ups with actors for the battle scenes. And the duel, because Larry – Mr Olivier – wasn't fit enough after that bang on his mouth.'

'He's still determined to fight it himself?'

'So they say.'

The first need, clearly, was to explore the area. I had been invited by Angeline's mother to return with her for supper. As soon as I could I busied myself in the garden shed, pumping up the tyres of the absent Mr Byers's bicycle, mending a puncture in one of them and greasing the chain, etcetera. Angeline had a bicycle in working order, though she did not seem very enthusiastic about cycling very far while the weather was so hot.

'What's it in aid of?' asked her mother as I came back into the house, which was a modest semi-detached, as the English define such dwellings, in a cul-de-sac behind which lay some woods.

'To see something of this beautiful part of England, Mrs Byers,' I said.

'I'd hardly call it that. The suburbs, that's what it is. We lived in Holland Park before we went abroad, you know. That was more like it.' She was a thin woman with a rather unsatisfied look about her. She smoked cigarettes nervously, and often had a glass in her hand. 'You'll have a drink now?'

'As soon as I have washed my hands, Mrs Byers.'

'I put a clean towel out.'

After supper Angeline proposed that she and I might stroll along to the pub, as she called it. After the rough bars of Enniskerry this was a rather more respectable establishment. The low-ceilinged rooms were thronged; other people stood out in the small garden. On such a warm summer's evening the men wore open-necked shirts and the women quite flimsy frocks. Of course, there were many in uniforms, including some Americans.

'It is pleasant here,' I told Angeline.

'Not bad.'

'But not as nice as Japan?' I asked, attempting to resume a conversation from the supper table. Mrs Byers had spoken of their time in the East and I had been rather startled by Angeline's enthusiasm for Japan and all things Japanese. But she did not seem to want to return to the subject. 'Oh, never mind that now,' she said impatiently. Her eyes strayed round the scene, I noticed, as if searching for someone.

A number of young people presently came over. They were from the tennis club, Angeline explained, as she perfunctorily introduced me. One fellow was in the air force, about to be sent to Canada for pilot training. I would like to have questioned him about this scheme and the long-term planning of the English war effort it indicated, but did not wish to appear too inquisitive.

'What are you in?' he was asking.

'Oh, I am simply an Irishman who has come over here to join up if I can – '

'But you told me you have already been invalided out,' interrupted Angeline.

Damn! I thought her too busily talking to another man to have noticed what I was saying.

'Now my head is so much better I don't see why I should not re-enlist,' I replied.

'Frederick was injured by a shot from the *Bismarck*,' said Angeline loudly.

'Really?' asked the one to whom she had been talking. 'What ship?'

'The *Prince of Wales*, old chap.'

Immediately he began asking all sorts of questions. He was a little older than the others, and wearing a dark-blue blazer. I suspected that he might be a naval officer on leave.

'I'm afraid I don't remember a single thing about it,' I said. 'The infernal knock on the head saw to that.'

He persisted in general questions about people I might have known, and places I should have known. Luckily, a mention of Esmond Knight turned the conversation into safer ways. Angeline told stories of the filming in Ireland to which all her friends listened, though not without making remarks of a foolish or philistine nature.

'Laurence Olivier,' said one. 'Isn't he the chap who blubbed in *Fire Over England*?' And when they learned that the film was from the play by Shakespeare, another fellow groaned, 'Oh God, back to school!' and the rest began to pretend to sleep and make snoring noises.

'It's their way,' said Angeline when I walked with her to her house. 'They make a joke of everything like that.'

'A strange kind of joke, to mock their country's greatest poet and one of the filmworld's finest actors.'

'Oh, you don't understand us. You don't seem to understand us at all.'

Naturally, I sought to make amends and profess what 'good types' they all were, but she remained distant.

Though the sun was now setting it was still very warm, without a breath of wind. 'We should take a swim now,' I suggested as we came to her house.

'We were all afternoon swimming.'

'But at night it is different. It is romantic. The water envelopes the body as silk. One should be, as the Germans say, *nackt in der Nacht*.'

'What does that mean?'

'As it sounds: with nothing on at night.'

'Ah, you should see me in the moonlight sometimes. I flit down through the wood – we've got our own path to the back of the Ac, you know. Sneak in when it's close and no one's there. It's lovely.'

'There will be a moon tonight.'

'I told you. I couldn't swim another stroke.'

'Tomorrow night!'

'We'll see.'

'Oh Angeline, you are so beautiful.'

She pushed me away. 'Please don't.'

'Why not?'

'Because.'

'Because of what?'

'Because of all sorts of things, but mainly that I am engaged. It's not fair on Derek.'

I was crushed. 'But you have not mentioned any Derek before,' I blurted out. 'Not at any time.'

'You see, he is a prisoner. Of the Japanese. I have only had one letter in the last year.'

'I am truly sorry, dear Angeline. I will see you tomorrow.' What else could a soldier say?

According to the map, Denham was not more than five miles, or eight kilometres, from Rickmansworth, but Angeline proposed that we should wend our way by a more picturesque route. I had arrived early, impatient to be off, and been obliged to wait until she descended. But when she finally appeared my heart turned over! She wore pleated shorts, a short-sleeved blouse and a yellow ribbon to tie her hair back. Her long slim legs were bare, her feet in sandals.

We passed through small villages of thatched cottages and duckponds, a different England from such memories as I had of travels with my father. There was little traffic on the road other than military vehicles. Each lorry laden with troops passed with shouts and whistles for Angeline. Once the soldiers were all singing at the tops of their voices, and the song they sang was our 'Lili Marlene'.

'You disliked being Angeline who danced on the village green,' I said to her. 'Imagine what it could be like to be a Lili Marlene.'

'Did you know one?' she asked, in a tone of voice I had not heard exactly before, almost a challenge.

We came at last to Denham, a village more picturesque than any previously seen, with cottages and inn grouped around a central green and a small river running past. The Angeline of the song would have been quite at home here. I could not believe that film studios could be anywhere in the vicinity, but after a break to enjoy a glass of 'shandy' and eat the sandwiches which Mrs Byers had provided, we continued only a little way before vast buildings hove into view. I counted three imposing concrete and glass blocks, close to the road, and beyond them what I instantly recognized as a vast sound stage, together with all the other buildings that spring up where films are made.

As we slowly cycled on, the full extent of the lot became apparent. It must have enclosed sixty hectares at least, with wooded as well as open ground, the same river running through the grounds and, at the far end, a great house from times past.

'That's where Korda lives,' Angeline said.

'Sir Alexander Korda?'

'When he's here, that is. He's been in America for ages. He has a flat in the house, they say, with a butler, a cook and a housekeeper. I think the writers also work there.'

I looked at the mellow red-brick mansion with longing. Oh, to be back among the litter of paper and stylos and typewriters and coffee cups along the scenario corridor. Oh, if only Goebbels's vision could be realized, and our two countries – my two countries – join together to give the world such power and prosperity as it had never known. Unfortunately, the news these days was chiefly of the bullfrog Mussolini, imprisoned by fellow Italians who had newly recovered their bravery. He had been a dubious asset for too long, but such a humiliation would not be helpful to our cause. No more encouraging were the English claims about the damage inflicted on Hamburg during a season of great night raids. Making every allowance for their exaggerations, it sounded bad.

We cycled on for a time. The road from the studios was also the main road back to Rickmansworth. Now, even more lorries of troops went waving and whooping by.

'Soon I shall become one of these fellows,' I said to Angeline with a smile, 'but while I await my papers I should try to find some work as an "extra" again. How does one do that at Denham?'

'I've no idea.'

'No need to snap my head off,' I said. 'You must have met many such persons in your work.'

She cycled in silence for a while, then spoke. 'There is someone, actually. You saw him at the Ac.'

'The Ac?'

'The Aquadrome. Where we went yesterday.'

'Ah, the fellow who knows about horses.'

'Yes. He's called Jacko.'

'Where would one find him?'

She looked a little shy. 'We could see if he's at his caravan if you like.'

'Of course!'

We had to go back a little way before turning off up a narrow lane. From the lane we went on to an even lesser road, with deep ruts from cart and tractor wheels which had baked hard in the summer heat. We dismounted and pushed our bicycles. At last we came to signs of human habitation. I would not describe it as an idyllic retreat. There were some derelict farm buildings, a pile of worn tyres, an old charabanc without its wheels, a wooden cabin with shuttered windows and, in the shade of a clump of trees, a caravan painted gay colours such as I had seen in depictions of gipsy life.

The man called Jacko came swaggering towards us. He was perhaps five years older than me. His ears, I noticed, were angled like those of a fawn and in one of them was a small gold ring. His teeth were very white as he flashed a smile of welcome.

'I thought I recognized those long legs,' he said to Angeline.

'This is a friend from Ireland, Fred Harris.'

'How do you do, Fred Harris?'

We shook hands. I noticed now the silver buckle on the broad leather belt which held his trousers, and the curls of hair on his chest as revealed by a shirt unbuttoned to the waist. Certainly he had a *braggadocio* to him, but I was sure he was of gipsy blood, as distasteful as that of Jews.

Could he offer us some beer, he asked. Angeline said she'd sooner have tea. I murmured as discreetly as possible that after the beer we had already taken outside the Denham inn what I most desired was a visit to the lavatory.

'Help yourself,' he said, waving a hand to indicate the surrounding landscape. 'As long as you don't stay too close.'

When I returned from the concealment of a tree some way off, they were sitting by the caravan, he on an old car seat, she on a cabin chair. Another cabin chair was set aside for me. A kettle heated on a spirit stove.

'Angeline tells me you're after some crowd work on "Henry Vee"?'

It took me a moment to decipher what he meant. 'That is so,' I said. 'If that is the next film to be in progress.'

'They start next Monday.'

'You work at the studios?' I pretended to want to know.

'From time to time,' he said with his raffish smile.

'What do you do?'

'Things with horses, that kind of thing.'

'You're a stunt man?'

'Sometimes, if it's not too dangerous,' he grinned again. 'If I wanted to get killed, I'd be in the army or the navy, wouldn't I?'

'Oh, you always say that,' said Angeline sharply. 'He broke his back in a circus fall, and one leg's crooked. He was turned down for the forces.'

'Or so it says on my bit of paper,' said Jacko with a wink. 'Which is more than most of them can produce as hangs around for a day's work on the set.'

'How do you mean?'

'Best not to ask. There's not too many able-bodied men left around, what with the call-up and the war work.'

'So who are they?'

'Deserters, the most of them. Army, navy, merchant seamen, even a couple of Yanks. But don't go putting that about.'

It was more than I had dared hope, to have such an expert entrée. Jacko promised to take me along when the time came. More immediately, or as soon as we had drunk strong black tea, there was much talk of horses to endure, and the inspection and admiration of the tall grey gelding which Jacko kept, along with some pigs, in a triangle of rough land adjoining the encampment. I had had more of my share of horses in Ireland, but reflecting that one never knew what might be useful, I made myself interested.

While Angeline cantered round the field a few times on the horse, I took the opportunity to come to the point with friend Jacko. He listened without taking his eyes off horse and rider, and continued to shout words of advice or approval.

'To lodge with me, and no questions asked, two pounds the week,' he said after a minute's thought. 'For the instruction and the use of the horse, ten shillings a time. For getting you taken on at the studios, ten pounds.'

I pretended to weigh this up. 'I shall be after my money's worth!'

'Done!' he said, and we smote hands.

Angeline came in, flushed and excited from her exercise and seeming oblivious to the chafing her bare legs must have suffered from pressing the horse's sides. As she slithered off its back, Jacko caught her round the hips and set her down with a flourish. I felt a pang of jealousy.

'Show us some of your circus tricks, Jacko,' she cried. 'He can do the most hair-raising things, like hanging on right down Prince's side as he gallops along, or standing on his back.'

'Not now,' laughed Jacko. 'Too hot for that kind of thing.' One hand still rested familiarly on her rump.

It was indeed hot as at last we cycled back to Rickmansworth. The road had absorbed the sun's fierce rays all day and was now like the top of a stove. My face and the back of my neck burned, and my arms were a bright red. It would be good to have a late swim, I suggested again, but Angeline retorted that she was far too 'whacked'. Next morning she had to resume at the studios, and simply had to have an early night.

After supper at my hotel I strolled back to her street and found a small path through the woodland behind the houses. It led me eventually to a high fence. At one point someone had made a gap in it. On the other side basked the lake, now deserted. This must be where she came.

On the way back, I slipped quietly into the garden and 'borrowed' Mr Byers's bicycle again. It would be useful.

He was a good instructor, that Jacko, if a hard one. He taught me to stay on his horse without hands even when it reared on its hind legs or danced sideways. He taught me to swing a sword and wield a club while it did so. With himself mounted on another nag he borrowed, we fought a few duels. I was black and blue within two days from many falls and the odd thwack or kick. And there had I been resolving never to sit on one of the beasts again!

'What's it all in aid of?' he asked as we drank beer

and smoked our pipes the first evening.

'Please?'

'What is it for, all this effort?'

'To win my spurs, of course, old man.'

'Your spurs!' He made a rasping noise with his lips. 'I told you, there's only one or two days with horses, and neither of those needing more than a handful of riders. You'll be lucky to get five days leaning on a spear.'

'There is still the duel between the King and the Constable.'

'Mr Olivier is riding himself as the one. I am the other.'

I took a drink of beer. 'That is what I have been meaning to ask you,' I said. 'I want to take your place.'

He stared at me for an instant before shaking his head in elaborate disbelief. 'Is that all?' he cried. 'You wouldn't care to borrow my balls while you're about it?' But in that stare before he spoke I had seen such a pack of jostling apprehensions, calculations, speculations that I knew I had a chance.

'It is a hard fall,' I said, 'that the Constable has to take, if I read the camera script correctly. Flat on his back from a rearing horse, in full armour.'

'It is the job.'

'But you have broken so many bones already.'

He shrugged.

'If you are taken into hospital, might that not be awkward?'

'What do you mean?'

'Questions asked, papers to be produced.'

He flushed. 'I am no stinking deserter – '

'Of course you are not. But nor are you in war work. You are not at a factory line or in the fields or down a mine, as is required. Think what they will make of your fine little hideaway here, the bureaucrats with their forms and their regulations.'

He seemed to nod.

'You are a gipsy, aren't you, Jacko? Officials always think the worst of gipsies. It is the same everywhere.'

He put another match to his pipe, still not speaking.

'Let me wage the duel for you. You can have a small accident while practising. Or have burned your hand on your stove.'

Now he spoke, quietly. 'Why are you so bloody anxious to help me, Harris? What's in it for you?'

I looked him squarely in the eye. 'I will tell you if you give me your word as a gentleman not to tell Miss Byers.'

'Angeline?' He looked surprised.

'Angeline is why I must acquit myself with honour in combat, and take that fall like a man. I am in love with her, old chap. I tell you, it is the real thing. I cannot sleep at night for thinking of her. I have sometimes let myself believe that she is not altogether horrified by my attentions, but she cannot respect me. You have heard her talk of the shooting in Ireland, when I was cast in such a lowly role and made the butt of jokes – '

'It was a picture! Who cares?'

'In the filmworld, everyone. It is a small model of the real world, with its officers and its soldiers, its heroes and its clowns. And if I am to win Angeline I must play a swagger part just once.'

He looked at me for a long time before replying. Finally he said, 'I could tell you two or three things about Angeline.'

'They would make no difference.'

He pondered again. 'I would need recompensing.'

'Of course.'

We arranged the terms over another bottle. After Jacko had retired to his caravan I sat on until it began to get dark, then wheeled Mr Byers's bicycle down the track and set off for Rickmansworth, and the Aquadrome.

Two nights I kept vigil without reward, unless you count the spectacle at sunset once of a scrawny man and a fat woman towelling one another after disporting in the water. They must have been at least fifty years of age. It was quite disgusting. Late on the third night, when I was telling myself that in another five minutes I would leave, I heard a faint sound from the direction of the path through the woods. I held my breath. The moonlight seemed to turn the scene into a photographic negative, with the shapes of the trees brightly silvered against the enclosing blackness. The surface of the lake shimmered. There were the usual small sounds of nature in such places, the faint plop of a fish or frog, but not this other sound again.

Suddenly there was movement. She emerged from the wood about two hundred metres away from me, on the other side of the narrow end of the lake. There was no mistaking the quite tall figure, the pale hair and the striped towelling robe. She kicked sandals from her feet, then loosened the tie of the robe. My heart seemed to be beating inside my skull. She tossed the robe aside and began to wade into the water.

Never had I seen such beauty. She could have been a goddess of the ancient world. I waited until she had reached swimming depth before wriggling out of my own clothes and creeping as silently as I could into the lake. The water felt like warm milk. I struck out, using a careful breast stroke rather than the crawl, and must have approached within sixty metres before alarming her. She did not call out but immediately began to swim frenziedly for the shore. I shouted, 'It is I, Friedrich!' but she thrashed on. Only as she began to flounder ashore did she look back. 'Angeline,' I cried.

She turned, covering her breasts with her hands. The water came up to her belly just below the navel. 'What are you doing here? Where did you come from?'

'I was about to enjoy a solitary midnight swim when I saw a naiad approach.'

'You were spying on me.'

'No,' I continued edging slowly towards her. She moved back and now the water reached only to that quarter that is the glory of woman. One hand moved instinctively there. I followed and stood facing her.

'What do you want?' She was shivering.

'Only to know what I have done wrong, that you should have become so different to me in the last days?'

She opened her mouth as if to reply, but only sighed.

'Is it the man Jacko? Is there something concerning him and yourself that I must not know? Because I do not believe for one moment in this Derek who has come between us so late in the day! Why had I not heard of him before? He does not exist!'

'He does! Oh, Christ, he exists all right, in Officers' Camp, Penang, care of the International Red Cross, and makes me feel guilty and I can't even remember what he looks like and Jacko makes it worse and now you make it worse again. Who are you, what are you trying to do? Tom, who was the one in the pub the other night with a blue blazer and was talking to you about the navy – he's in the navy, sub-lieutenant – he said you were talking utter rubbish and must be a deserter or a spy.'

'Neither! I have told you – '

'Then why did you call out your name as Friedrich only a minute ago?'

'It was merely a joke. In any case, if you admire the Japanese so much, you ought also to keep an open mind about their allies.'

'Oh, God, you don't understand us at all, do you? What's all this skulduggery with Jacko about getting work on the film again? Why's that so important?'

She was shivering, and not from any cold. I yearned to enfold her in my arms. But before I could speak she continued.

'Already there have been men asking questions,' she said.

'What men? What kind of questions?'

'About that photographer friend of yours. When did you last see him, that sort of thing. Can't you see it will look suspicious, you turning up again? No one else has come from Ireland except a couple of horses. People will think it's something to do with me.'

'Then they will be right! Tomorrow they shall see me acquit myself with honour, and win your heart at last.'

'What?'

'I am fighting the duel in Jacko's stead. He has – '

'No!' Her cry echoed across the lake.

'Be quiet,' I urged.

She was shaking her head so hard her hair swished from side to side. She spread her arms beseechingly, regardless of her nakedness. 'Please don't. Stay away. Please . . .'

'But why?'

'I don't know. Just stay away, that's all.' Her voice was strained.

'Very well,' I said. 'If it matters so much to you, I will go back to Jacko and tell him that all we have arranged is not to be.'

'Promise.'

'I promise,' I said. I bent down suddenly and scooped her up, one hand grabbing her round the shoulders, the other hooked behind her knees. For an instant she reposed in my arms. I drank in the freckles that covered her body, the patch of tawny hair. From some instinctive reflex, or perhaps from something more, one arm of hers wrapped round my neck. Oh, the elastic softness of her skin! I could have sold the world for it.

Instead I cried, 'Good! That is settled, now we swim.' I charged with her back into the lake, whooping. She laughed despite herself and clutched me tighter, until I was out of my depth and turned over to trundle noisily on my back with my hands cupped round her breasts. She squirmed free and trod water while I made her laugh again, duck-diving and bobbing up again and generally showing my white rump to the moon.

Then I drowned her. It was not easy. I do not believe it could ever be easy, even if one did not love and desire the person. She thrashed and fought. That beautiful body lashed against me. I kept one hand locked over her mouth, but still she screamed. Her fingernails tore deep gouges all over me. But at last she floated inertly, face down. I towed her to the centre and left her to sink into the depths.

There was no other way. She guessed too much. She would be at the studios to point and tell. In the filmwar we were soldiers on opposite sides, and one of us had to pay the price. But, as I floundered ashore, foul tastes rose into my mouth and I fell to my knees to retch and groan and heave up litres of bitter fluid. Of course, in the struggle I had swallowed much stagnant brown water.

At some point in it, also, she had bitten my finger at the root of the nail. In the weeks that followed a discolouration like the map of some small island of the Antilles, red and black and purple, slowly appeared as the nail grew, a fraction more each day. When it should all have grown out again, I promised myself, I would be free of what I had done.

Eleven

Half the morning I had nothing to do but spin my thumbs on the edge of the lot. Jacko had fulfilled his bargain. I had arrived at the studios to find myself expected, and no questions asked. But the actor Leo Genn who was to portray the Constable of France needed to leave as early as possible, since he was not yet formally released from the army, and the one shot in which the Constable raised his vizor had therefore to be obtained first.

Why this should have taken so long I could not tell, other than from the general experience that every shot takes a small part of eternity. If God had created the world as a movie, it would have occupied Him for seven centuries rather than seven days. I could only fret in the sun that was already hot and try to overcome the horror of what I had done, the terror of what I still had to do.

The location was a small field some way north of the studios, within view of the road along which Angeline and I – dear God, Angeline – had pedalled so few days earlier. Normally it was the pasture of a few cows said to belong to the film tycoon Korda.

They had been temporarily moved elsewhere, leaving much evidence of their tenancy.

The other extras were, as Jacko had said, a despicable bunch who could only too easily be deserters and petty criminals. At least they were incurious about me. Perhaps it was the law among this riff-raff never to ask questions of each other.

The danger of recognition, I estimated, was greatest from those who might remember me as a man and not merely as an extra – the continuity girl Joan, for example. With luck, however, I should not come close to her until I rode before the camera, by which point I planned to be safely helmeted. Krasker and his crew need not see me until that time, either. Olivier? Our encounter *vis-à-vis* had been in a dimly-lit caravan. Besides, he would be preoccupied with securing this crucial scene.

I would not be requiring make-up, thank God – I doubt that I could have borne the touch of soft hands that would only remind me of soft hands now perished.

That left the wardrobe assistant, and the almost certain chance that she would have at one time or another fussed over my aluminium-painted chain mail or soup-plate helmet in Ireland.

At last I saw the figure in the black armour of the Constable walk stiffly away from the activity around the camera towards the dressing tent. I waited until he had gone in, and followed.

The girl had red hair and a shy manner and yes, she had been in Ireland. She was poring over a typewritten list.

'Mr Jackman?' she asked, which was the name

Jacko went by. 'Mr Genn is just getting out of the costume.'

I had an idea and began immediately to take of my clothes. Embarrassed, she looked away. 'Excuse me,' I said, 'but I guess it will be hot in that damned iron suit today.'

'It damned well is,' came a voice from behind the curtain which screened off the rear of the tent. 'And I had only to sit on the horse and look keenly into the middle distance. You have to go three rounds with Larry.'

'Or better, a knockout,' I called back. I stripped down to a strange garment used by players of cricket and football to protet their manhood. Jacko had insisted I should wear it, also a thick shirt and long drawers. That part of his advice I ignored. As they were passed out to me, I pulled on the chain mail, hauberk and chausses over my bare skin. The cuirass and pauldrons and other steel pieces were buckled over these. Finally my head was enclosed in the cruel, plumed helmet with the snout of a medieval devil. Now I was safe: even with the vizor raised, my face was shadowed; with it down, no one could know me.

Genn emerged, fastening the last button of his uniform. He seemed an affable fellow. 'Rather you than me,' he said. 'Good luck!'

The armourer handed me my sword and shield and knelt to fix my spurs. 'For Gawd's sake don't use them,' he said, 'or we'll have the veterinary inspector down on us.'

With his help I heaved myself into the saddle. I could feel the weight of my armour, but the black brute of a stallion seemed hardly to notice his burden.

'And better not connect with this either,' added the armourer – 'this' being the mace which he was hooking over the pommel of my saddle. I tried it in my grip. It sat well in the gauntlet. The head was heavy and studded with spikes. Man could slay a giant with such a weapon.

I jog-trotted up to the camera site and the throng of people around it. Olivier came striding towards me in his gleaming silver armour, only his helmet removed. His eyes were angry.

'Where have you been?' he snarled. 'We've been kicking our heels for half an hour.'

'But I have only had the armour as Mr Genn has taken it off –'

'I can't hear you. Lift your vizor, man!'

I did so, keeping hold of it so that my mailed fist might mask at least part of my features.

Olivier stared. 'You are not Jacko,' he said at last.

'He is not well. He sent me instead.'

'Haven't I seen you before somewhere?'

'Never that I remember.'

'Your name?' he persisted.

'Mack.'

'Very well, Mr Mack. We'll see what you're made of.'

So, of course, things could not have gone worse. We were shooting only preliminary circlings and thrusts in the duels, but each time something went wrong. By the time Olivier reluctantly called the lunch break we still had not clashed steel upon steel. I turned the horse over to a groom to be watered and tethered in the shade, collected a plateful of food and clanked to a spot where I could be alone. As I picked my way through the other extras some sneered and one called out sardonically, 'Thanks mate, you'll have us on overtime yet.'

At least I could wrench off my helmet here and put on my glasses. The sun played on the rest of the armour like a blow-torch. I felt the sweat trickling in rivulets. The scratches Angeline had made stung and itched. Places where the chain mail chafed bare skin were already painfully sore.

Suddenly I hated Olivier. I hated him for his arrogance. I hated him for not accepting the fine offer I had brought him. I hated him for this whole insane adventure, what it had already cost me and what was still to be claimed. All to the good: it should be an honest grudge fight now.

I saw a figure coming towards me and reached for the helmet. But it was no one I yet recognized. He was debonair, in short-sleeved shirt with a cravat at the neck, a panama hat on his head. He walked with short steps and eyes lowered, as if short-sighted. He carried a glass in one hand. As I watched, he had to pick his way through the extras who sprawled on the ground in the jerkins and hose of English foot-soldiers. His foot caught against one fellow's boot and he nearly tripped. Instead of trying to help, the wretch began swearing in what sounded like an American accent. 'Jesus, are you blind or something?'

He continued in this vein while the newcomer attempted to apologize. I forced myself to my feet and lumbered towards them. Why, why, why? It

197

was only inviting more trouble. I could not help it, that was why. Or did I already know?

'Leave him alone!' I shouted. 'Can you not see that his eyes have been injured?'

The fellow shut up and the assailed one came on towards me. One small ravaged eye was screwed in concentration, the other false. He said, 'But you are not Leo. I thought I would bring a drink for Leo.'

'Mr Genn had to go. I am his fight stand-in.'

'Then you must have the drink – or what is left of it. I'm afraid I spilled most of it when I tripped. Thank you, by the way, for speaking up for me with our friends there.'

'They are scum.'

He squinted at me again. 'I know you, don't I?'

'I think not.'

'But evidently you know who I am.'

I had a dull feeling that I was a player in a scenario fashioned by one of these fusspot screen writers who must tie together every strand in the story. The figure with whom he began had now to reappear and preside over the climax. 'Captain Fluellen', I quoted, 'you must come directly to the mines.'

'Hah!' The patched-up face formed itself into a fierce smile. 'An educated stand-in. Esmond Knight is obliged to you.'

'Mack,' I said. 'They call me Mack.'

He peered close at me again. 'Nonsense. You're no Mack. You don't look like a Mack. More like a Max, if anything. We have met, you know. Can't remember where. It'll come back to me.' He looked round the scene, the small field, the bright colours of the English tents which had been set up again, the

198

litter of a film unit. 'Don't you get the feeling there is something funny about today? Look at the light for a start.'

There was indeed a curious coppery glare to the sun, so that every colour seemed to be intensified. No breath of wind stirred the air.

'It is just like the dream I used to have, before I got this eye back. Often had it, always the same. There was this battlefield with knights in armour, little tents just like those, bodies all over the place and a bloody great red sun in the sky. I had to get to the King and warn him – and that was where it all went a bit Salvador Dali – I had to tell him that Number Two gun was knocked out and the chief gunner's mate as dead as could be, his head a pulp, which was crazy on a medieval battlefield, but there you are. The *angst* bit was real enough, seeing the King on his white steed and not being able to get to him, the old feet stuck in glue like they always are in a dream . . .'

He paused for a moment. 'Don't know why I'm telling you all this. To tell the truth, no need for me to be here today. Not called. Got the days mixed up and now I have to wait until my chap comes for me again. But it's bloody weird, that dream, isn't it? The weirdest thing of all was that I was having it long before Larry phoned and I even knew about this film.'

I said, 'I think I must make ready now.'

'Of course, of course, old chap. Sorry if I bored you. I'll try to remember where we met.'

We faced each other again, the King and I. In the

script I had studied so often twelve separate sequences made up the actual duel, of which only three were yet in the can. The one I awaited could not come until the end. Perhaps three hours of usable light remained, less if the strange feverish sun presaged a storm.

Olivier began to explain what was required from me in the first piece of action.

'You can save this time,' I said, cutting him off. 'I know what is wanted.'

His eyes flashed with anger – he wore no vizor and his whole face could be seen. 'Do you generally tell the director what he should or should not do?'

I pointed my sword to the sun. 'Do you want to complete this shoot today?'

He continued to stare at me for a span, then abruptly wheeled his white horse away to confer with Krasker and Hildyard and the cutter Beck who stood in as director. He returned with another violent manoeuvre of the luckless beast. 'Very well, but be it on your own head if you get it wrong.'

He jockeyed into position to come thundering into the arena of turf before the camera. Around it, in the imagination of the scenarist, the English soldiers were to gather and cheer on their King in what they sensed was the final match of the battle. Not that these wretched extras were disposed to show enthusiasm for anything.

All right: we would give them something to stir them up. I took up station facing Olivier across the circle.

He came at me with sword upraised. I was to parry the cut with my shield and take a chop at him as he passed. In this shot it did not have to connect realistically; there would be a close-up of the blow to follow.

The first take was nearly enough. My shield took his sword with a fine smack. But Olivier thought my counter-stroke came some piddling fraction of a second too late. 'It'll be all right,' said Krasker; Olivier still insisted on another try.

This time I struck sooner. Olivier delayed his duck out of the way by the same particle of time. The sword was a filmsword, not sharp enough to do any real harm, but it caught him hard on the side of what was only a filmhelmet. When you see him in the movie reeling in the saddle, almost falling, that was this take, and he was not acting.

There was a hush. Beck it was, I guess, who called out, 'Are you all right, Larry?' He hauled himself up. The white horse trotted round in a loop and brought him back towards me. There was a fine dent in the helmet and a piece sliced out of the encircling crown. Olivier's face was contorted with pain.

He mouthed to me, 'I shall not forget that.'

He was as good as his word. In the next shot, or maybe it was the next but one, he had to disarm me with a blow to the sword wrist. He took me on the hand instead, which was perhaps not intended, but with a force that was. It felt as if he'd brought the edge of an iron spade down. The pain was so great that I screamed inside my iron mask, and for a moment the brightness beyond the slits in my vizor threatened to turn dark.

The two or twenty takes that followed – I truly

have no idea how few or how many there might have been – remain only as a confused impression. At least one hour must have passed. I seem to remember some of the usual technical delays: aircraft flying overhead, a film jam in the camera. It was hotter than ever. I stewed like a knuckle of veal inside my armour. Every weal and raw place on my body smarted. My hand throbbed.

My turn came to disarm the King. I was not armed with the mace in my left hand. With it, I was supposed to parry another attack from him and knock the sword from his grasp. I sent it spinning savagely, but without touching Olivier. This was not the occasion.

The occasion would be the next shot, which was the same small piece of action from a different angle and continued beyond the striking of the sword from the King's grasp. He was not to lose his balance for an instant and lurch before me. I was to raise the mace on high, ready to smash it down on his head.

The script then called for the King to straighten up and, with a backhander from his mailed fist, send the Constable flying. The script this once would not be obeyed. All I had to do was strike one beat ahead of Olivier and that would be the end of him and the end of my mission.

There was a pause while they changed the film magazines. Someone brought me a cold drink. No longer caring if I were recognized, I tipped the vizor back to take it. Hildyard was busy with the camera. Olivier leaned down to confer with Krasker and Beck.

I looked about me. The light was more feverish than ever. To the west, a black cloud filled the sky. I picked out Esmond Knight's panama hat among a knot of bystanders. He waved and seemed to be trying to make some signal. Closer to hand, the extras had remained in position around the duelling ground, as if waiting for something. I guessed they had smelled the blood in the air.

To the east, the balloons above London shone like beads of mercury. A convoy of armoured cars crawled along the road.

The war, the war.

I dropped the vizor with a clang. We took our places.

'Who will take a bet on the Constable?' yelled a wag among the foot-soldiers. Beck screamed for silence. They ran the camera. The clapper boy marked the shot: 'Scene 243, Take 1'.

Olivier came storming. I knocked the sword from his grasp again. He lurched as directed. I kicked down against the stirrups and swung the mace up on outstretched arm. This was it! At which point the bastard hit me. Without waiting, without counting, he uncoiled a swing from the depths of his reach to its zenith.

You can see it all in the film, up to and including the fine performance by the extra who had been briefed to grab the black stallion and calm it.

His mailed fist – no wonder it gave its name to the *Panzerfaust* anti-tank weapon of our infantry – took me in the snout of my helmet, driving it against my face and hurling me from the saddle.

With the weight of the armour, I gathered the

momentum of a tank falling from a bridge. I landed flat on my back. There was a sound of many waterfalls in my ears and this time I did black out.

When I came round, they had the vizor open and the ambulance man was mopping my face. There was blood pouring from one eyebrow where my glasses had smashed into it, there was blood coming from my mouth.

Olivier's face was thrust into vision. 'Are you all right, old chap?'

I was too numbed to reply, numbed in mind as well as body. For so much excitement and fear and steeling of oneself to have ended thus was worse than failure. It was nothing. Zero. Null.

They hauled me to my feet. My limbs did not seem broken, merely ground into butcher's *Wurst*. I rested for a while, exploring my teeth with my tongue to discover if they were loosened. One lens of my glasses, amazingly, was unbroken. I watched a black motor car come bumping in through the gate at the far end of the field. And gradually small scraps of overheard argument and covert glances in my direction to suggest that all might not be lost after all.

Olivier was saying it was all right, they could manage with what they had. Beck was sticking his heels in with a determination I hadn't seen in him before. 'You swung too soon, Larry. We'll have nothing of the club poised ready to crash down on you.'

'Cheat it, Reg, cheat it. I know you can.'

'I can't, Larry. I need it for the cut.' He appealed to Krasker. 'Aren't I right?'

Krasker looked in my direction again. 'The question is whether our friend there can oblige.'

'Naturally,' I shouted, even if nothing could have seemed harder at this moment.

'Right,' said Krasker. 'I smell about five minutes' light left.'

Extras, cursing, lifted me into the saddle. My sores burned inside the armour, the helmet was an intolerable weight. The black car was pulling up by the litter of gear behind the camera. Two men got out.

'I say, old chap, a swig of this might do wonders.' It was Esmond Knight squinting up at me. 'This' was a drink flask with the cap already removed. I drank. It was spirit flavoured with some strong aromatic. It stung the lesions in my mouth but diffused strength into my sinews. I took another gulp. What was holding us up now? Where had Olivier got to? Hell and damnation, he was leaning down to listen to one of the men who had got out of the car. Even as I watched, he shot a glance in my direction. And now the continuity girl Joan was pointing at me and saying something.

'Good God!' I heard close to hand.

I turned. It was Esmond Knight, his scarred face filled with astonishment.

'What is it?' I mumbled, still dazed.

'I remember, I remember!' he cried.

My hand tightened on the handle of the mace. I could silence him with one blow . . .

'Messenger boy, weren't you? Brought me a wire once?'

'You are mad,' I said.

Down the field another car was bumping towards the film site. But Olivier was riding back towards us.

'Listen, Larry, I know this fellow,' Knight cried. 'I knew I'd seen him somewhere before. It was at Ufa that time I made *Black Roses* – '

'Not now, Ned.'

'But it's important.'

'Not *now*, Ned!'

He addressed me. 'I don't know what the hell this is all about, but they want to talk to you. The chaps in the car there. They want to talk to you straight-away. But we'll go for a take first. All right?'

My reply was to close my vizor with a bang.

He sat stock still for a moment, then wheeled away. The camera was already running. If anyone marked 'Scene 243, Take 2', I did not see him.

The King came at me. I struck the sword from his hand again and swung the mace aloft to the very limit of my reach, my feet braced against the stirrups. Below me the bent head seemed to move on a notch at a time, as in a strip of film jerking frame by frame through the editing machine.

I could see each fine black corm of hair in the shaven skin of his neck, the tiny crater left by a spot. And my arm would not move.

'Cut!' Beck's voice sounded some infinite distance off. I became aware of sweat coasting down my sides.

Olivier was passing on in the same unearthly motion. I lowered the mace and looked around. The crowd was frozen. Esmond Knight held his mouth open, his finger pointing. The two men from the car were coming slowly towards me. Behind them, another car had arrived and from it, suddenly resuming the ordinary pace of the world, emerged a tall, gesticulating, unmistakable, untidy figure –

Martin! Martin Kilner.

There came a flash of lightning and a peal of thunder. My black stallion reared.

I stabbed spurs into flanks and he took off. We thundered up the field. Ahead loomed the hedgerow and just to the left – yes! – a five-barred gate. I had never jumped before. The horse was carrying a hundred kilogrammes of man and armour, but we cleared it like a Cossack and his steed.

Twelve

For perhaps three kilometres my gallant steed kept up his headlong progress while I devoted myself to hanging on. As soon as I felt him begin to flag, I let him ease to a walk and looked around. There were no signs of pursuit. I wrenched off the black helmet and tossed it into deep cover. Another flash of lightning lit up the now eerily dark landscape, another clap of thunder sounded immediately above my head.

I reined to a halt and unfastened the grieves which pinched my legs. Pauldrons and chausses followed. I dismounted to remove spurs, tin shoes, chain mail, hauberk and breeches. The horse I stripped of its bright trappings. Only the mace remained of my accoutrements. I hung it back on the pommel as some kind of talisman, I guess. Naked save for the vestigial garment Jacko had lent me, I hauled myself wearily back into the saddle, and at this moment the rain struck. It came sluicing down, cooling my body, washing away the sweat and soothing the raw, red places. I rode on through the storm, singing at the top of my voice the song that had been popular when I left Berlin, *'Es geht alles vorüber'*, or 'Everything Shall Pass'.

Why had I stayed my hand when Olivier's head was bent defencelessly below me, his helmet offering as little protection against the mace as a sparrow's eggshell against a magpie's beak? I did not know, then. All I knew was that a great burden had been lifted from me. All I wanted now was to quit the pretend world of actors and propagandists and join in this damned war as a proper soldier. If the British had taken me then and offered me a rifle or a tank, I believe I would have accepted.

I had only a general idea of the direction I should take, but luck remained on my side. After skirting a cornfield I thought I recognized the tower of a small church in the distance. The storm ceased as quickly as it had begun and the sun was warm on my skin again. I passed under a clump of trees and suddenly found myself almost on top of a group of farm-workers who were pitchforking straw bales on to a cart. What was more, they were women, with their hair tied by cotton scarves and breasts straining against drab cotton shirts.

Immediately they set up a great chorus of screams which soon changed to cat-calls and laughter and at least one crudity. I saluted the ladies and urged my horse, as best I could with bare feet, to hurry again. Within another half-hour, and without further encounter, I came to Jacko's hideaway.

He was sitting outside the caravan with a pot of tea, as I remembered him from that day we first met. He said, 'Usually it is the horse we mean when we speak of riding bare-back.'

'It was like being in a stove in that damned armour,' I said.

'A mug of tea, then.'

'Thank you.'

I let him come close and hand it up to me. I had to be careful. I kept one hand free to grab the mace if I needed it. But he only walked appraisingly round my mount before resuming his seat.

'What now?' he said.

'I shall be on my way.'

'How will you go?'

I drank some tea before replying.

'I have looked about me here. There is a motor-cycle under a sheet behind the cabin. It has no permit, I expect, nor petrol ration. But you have petrol in a can, I have also discovered.'

'What are you offering?'

'This horse.'

He laughed out loud.

'He led the charge at Agincourt,' I said indignantly.

'Did he so? I thought that was a black creature.'

'As this fellow is,' I started to say, but looking down I saw that I now bestrode a streaky grey. My bare legs, conversely, were quite black with the dye washed from his coat by the rain.

'His name is Punch,' said Jacko. 'He has taken part in the Crusades, the Charge of the Light Brigade and *Lorna Doone*. He is the best-known film horse in the business. My advice would be to turn him loose at once.'

We did just that, rubbing the beast down, watering him and sending him on his way with a slap to the rump. I fetched a pail of water and washed myself thoroughly before putting on clean clothes. The mace I slipped into a hiding place I had already established, under the cabin where it was supported on old railway timbers. Only then did I reopen our barter.

'All right,' I said, 'twenty pounds. And when I have finished with the machine, like the horse it shall be turned loose. Left outside a railway station, for example, so that if it really is yours, you have only to report it stolen and it shall be returned to you.'

'In gold sovereigns, of course?'

I stared at him. Clearly he would have rooted around in my possessions during my absence, but I had taken good care to secrete certain items where he would not easily find them.

'How should I have gold sovereigns?' I demanded.

'You seem to be the kind of stranger up to the kind of coming and going that might have gold to spend. Where *do* you come from, Mr Harris?'

'I ask no questions of you. Ask no questions of me.'

'Angeline said something about Germany.'

'Leave Miss Byers out of this!'

My voice must have held an authentic tremor. He regarded me without the smile this time. 'Twenty-five pounds,' he said finally.

'Agreed.'

The machine had to have its tyres pumped up and its sparking plugs cleaned and its chain greased. By the time all was ready, the sun was beginning to sink in the sky. It would be dark within two hours and the primitive lights on the motor-bike would have been poor enough without the sticky paper which masked them, but I was impatient to be off. I listened for the sounds of any vehicle approaching up the rough track.

'I will fry some bacon and potatoes to see you on your way,' Jacko said.

'That is kind.'

I packed my things quickly and, while he was busy with the frying pan, knelt to reach into the space beneath the cabin. I found the cache of sovereigns, documents, spare glasses, etcetera, straightaway. Only the mace I had tossed in later seemed to have disappeared –

'So that's where you hid the gold? I might have known.'

I jerked round. Jacko looked down at me. He held a shotgun pointing at my face.

'Don't move, Nazi bastard,' he said.

Had I been a filmworld hero, I would have made some suitable retort. In fact I was numbed by shock and disappointment. So much for my charmed life!

'You can have it all,' I heard myself croaking.

'I shall, never fear. But that's a bonus. Getting you is what matters.' He spoke quickly, always a sign of nervousness.

Sensing a faint chance after all, I said, 'I did not think you cared about such questions. I thought you and I were kindred spirits – '

'You thought wrong. And where is Angeline?'

'How should I know? I have not seen her since I came here – '

'Those scratches all over your body. No armour caused them.'

'That costume assistant – what is her name? The red-head? She demonstrates her passion in unusual ways – '

'You lie!'

My hand lit at last on the shaft of the mace. In my other hand I grasped the package containing the sovereigns.

I made as if to turn and rise to my feet, the weapon still concealed by the weeds which grew round the cabin.

'Stop there!' he shouted.

I brandished the package. 'Take it, let me go, say nothing,' I said as conspiratorially as I could. 'Why invite those in authority to ask questions? You might find yourself regarded as deserter or criminal rather than a hero – '

'Shut up!'

'At least you should have the spoils,' I said. Quite deliberately, as in slow motion, I tossed the heavy small parcel towards him.

Automatically, his eyes left me as he reached out to catch it. The shotgun barrel wavered in the same direction. I hurled the mace. It hit his knee only six or seven feet from me. He gasped in pain and nearly fell. As the gun fired I was already under the blast of shot, though I heard it whistle past. I retrieved the mace, used it to smash the gun from his hand and then brought it down on the side of his head. He fell like an animal in a slaughter-yard.

A spike on the mace had brought away a narrow triangle of skull on which the black curls still grew.

So I could do that, too. It was not squeamishness which had stopped me before. But there was a curious glassy unreality about all that had happened since the horror of the lake. And even that could not press down so heavily while many new sensations jostled for my attention.

I hauled the body into a patch of tall nettles, ate the bacon and potatoes directly from the frying pan and rinsed it clean. Fifteen minutes later I was heading north with a map in which all England was crammed into half a sheet of paper. From some-where came a dull confidence that I would find my destination.

Lady MacMorris slithered out of the 'four-poster' bed and went to the window to draw the curtains. It was an enormous window, at least six metres wide and two metres high, so she only pushed aside two of the heavy velvet drapes. Bright daylight blazed through the fine stuff of her nightdress, limning her body. I had averted my eyes earlier, fearing her to be as slack and unattractive as the old whore who plied her trade across the street from my apartment in Berlin, but now I could see with some satisfaction that she possessed a statuesque and not un-Aryan physique with broad hips and strong legs.

'What time is it?' I asked.

'Nearly twelve. I shall go down as soon as I have dressed, and after an appropriate interval have Gibson bring you some hot water. We shall have lunch and then see about getting you to Ireland, if that's what you really want.'

'It is imperative, Lady MacMorris – '

'Do call me Jane.' She had pulled on a robe-like garment of deep cerise as she turned; she really looked a handsome woman.

'It is imperative, Jane, if I am to prevent this foolishness by the dynamiters of the IRA. Only if I can reach the ear of Mr de Valera himself have I any chance of success. Just imagine the consequences if the fools achieve their aims. Churchill could attack the Free State, and our two countries – *your* two countries – will hate each other for another thirty years.'

'The only possibility is to go to Belfast,' she said.

'That is perfect. To cross from the six counties into the twenty-six is not difficult.'

As soon as she had gone, I jumped out of bed and hurried into the adjoining bathroom. It was still there, fallen behind the radiator, a file of papers to constitute the most amazing stroke of luck a man might dream for himself. I had leafed through the pages as I sat on the ancient WC at some interval in our span of love and sleep. It was quite clearly a part of the English-American plans to invade Europe, evidently left here by Lady MacMorris's unregarded husband. For all his drunken ways, Sir George was a brigadier on the General Staff. With this tucked into the seat of my trousers I could return to Germany a hero regardless of the success or failure of the Olivier plan.

'Gibson' turned out to be an elderly maidservant who looked at me disapprovingly. She brought hot water in a copper vessel. As I shaved myself I reflected that at last I had acquitted myself as a soldier of the Reich. Indeed I had acquitted myself four-fold: once in acquiring the plans and three times with Lady MacMorris.

'I take it,' she said as we ate a salad with Russian eggs, 'that you have no travel permit.'

'I'm afraid not,' I said carelessly. Obviously I dare not use Martin Kilner's again.

'That is difficult. We can only try the Yanks.'

'The Americans?'

'I can't promise, mind you.'

While she busied herself with the telephone, I strolled on to the terrace. The house was situated on the shore of a wide estuary looking across to the distant principality of Wales. The sands were covered with a green weed of some kind that made them resemble meadows laced with small waterways. Many sea-birds could be seen.

Now that escape began to be a small possibility and not just a dream, I felt anxiety rising again. I had to suppress a wild urge to rush down to the marshes and find a boat – any boat – that I might row across the sea to Ireland.

At last Jane reappeared to say that we should set off, though she still couldn't promise anything. The car, an elderly model of a make unfamiliar to me, waited at the front door, a servant at the wheel.

We headed away from the estuary for some miles, through rural scenery and small villages with timbered houses, then into more urban landscape with busy roads and factory chimneys.

The car seemed to crawl along ever more slowly. I was too tense now to make intelligent conversation. Finally we stopped outside the gates of what was evidently an American military establishment. Soldiers with white-painted helmets on their heads and white gaiters round their legs stood importantly on guard. We waited many minutes before we were waved inside and directed to a building sited – I could now see – close to the concrete runway of a large aerodrome. An officer of senior rank, I judged, was emerging. He saluted Lady MacMorris in rather casual fashion, I thought, and nodded in my direction.

He had a heavy gangster face, a cap with a leather peak. As he bent to address my benefactress in a low voice, I tried hard to pick up something of what he was saying, but, despite all the gangster movies I had seen, his growling delivery was too strange to my ears. Then he wrenched open her door and for what seemed an eternity they paced up and down in the sunlight.

Jane searched in her handbag, produced a small diary and a propelling pencil and evidently proposed some dates. The officer began to smile vigorously, and kissed her hand before saluting again. As he turned to go, he handed her an envelope.

'The things I do for Ireland,' she said as she came back to the car. 'All the colonel cares about is to set up some duck shooting on the marshes. But here's your documentation, as he calls it.' She gave me the envelope.

I kissed her warmly in farewell. Inside the building an under-officer with many elaborate stripes on his sleeve looked at the papers and said, 'You're the guy whose ship was torpedoed? That's really tough.' I nodded. There was another very long wait then, which gave me worse and worse pains, but finally we were called – myself and some dozen uniformed men – to board the plane. It was, I think, of the same type as that in which I had arrived in England only some twenty days before, but painted a drab green and without seats or other comforts. We sat on the cabin floor amid many crates and other stores. Only sound and sensation told us we were airborne.

Thirteen

It was October before I reached Berlin. As in the case of the outward journey, I shall omit any detailed itinerary. For one thing, I can no longer separate the long spells of waiting at different stages. I can recall that landing at the American base in Belfast produced further hazards, as this turned out to be the same field as the one occupied by the civil airport. Many English uniforms were to be seen. However, I managed to slip out by begging a ride into the city with an American lieutenant who had been a fellow passenger on the plane.

In Dublin I was obliged to throw my weight about both with our useless embassy and with the same IRA buffoons as I had been saddled with before. I let them have my indignation at their letting Martin Kilner escape. Can you believe it, they had some hen-and-bull story about a message from the Reich telling them the operation was called off?

Eventually the importance of the invasion plans in my possession permeated their thick hides, helped by the grand réclame of the rescue of Benito Mussolini from the Alpine prison in which his turncoat countrymen were holding him. This spectacular exploit by Otto Skorzeny, whom I had met at Friedenthal, impressed even the Irish. At once they began to mutter among themselves about organizing my return voyage.

Because my existence was now known to the secret police I had to remain in hiding in another suburban house, which made me depressed. Only when my departure was said to be imminent did I travel, disguised as a priest, to the southern harbour where I had arrived four months earlier. Here there was a further delay, during which I had to stay hidden in a hovel without light or habitation. At last I was smuggled aboard another fishing boat, and for three days was handsomely sea-sick.

This time there was no U-boat. The rendezvous was with a Breton fishing boat. Its crew was no less suspicious of me, nor more welcoming, than the Irish, but within a week I was in Brest, trying my damnedest to persuade the local commandant to send a *Fernschreib* to Berlin. No aircraft, I have to record, sped me on the last leg of my journey. I went by train, 2nd class. I finally stood before von Damitz on the day that the wretched Italian government of Marshall Badoglio had the insolence to declare war on its former allies, an event which had evidently affected von Damitz's reactions to my report. Certainly he seemed far less concerned about the failure to bring back Olivier than I had feared, if also less impressed by the military plans I had brought instead.

'So we have not our Europa-hero after all,' he said.

'I regret not, Herr Sturmbannführer.'

'Perhaps it is not too bitter a loss. Our attitudes must be re-examined in the light of the news from Italy. When our "allies" can desert us so easily, we should concentrate our efforts on showing them who is master rather than trying to impress them with our culture. You will have learned of the splendid exploit led by Sturmbannführer Skorzeny of this organization, when he snatched the rightful leader of the Italian people, and loyal friend of the Führer, from captivity?'

'The Irish were talking of nothing else, sir.'

'Exactly! There was a stroke of propaganda worth a thousand talking films.'

'My only ambition now is to become a soldier of the Reich . . .'

He was already fishing among the papers on his desk, oblivious to what I was trying to say. 'Ah, your secret invasion plans! To bring us such a present showed the right spirit, and I shall see that you are commended accordingly. Of course they are not to be taken too seriously. All our information is that the assault – should it ever materialize – will be across the Channel at its narrowest, that is to say it will aim to take the ports of Calais and Boulogne and Dunkirk. This talk of Normandy and of artificial harbours is what the English term a "red herring", I believe.'

He dropped the folder into the basket. 'As for your future employment, I understand that the ministry expects you to return to duties in the Film Division, though not necessarily as Filmadjudant to the Reichsminister.'

'But Herr Sturmbannführer, you have yourself

indicated that the time has arrived for real action rather than make-believe.'

He looked at me bleakly. 'You mean you wish to remain with this organization?'

'If the Sturmbannführer approves.'

'Then why did you not kill Olivier?'

All my rehearsed answers deserted me. I stammered something.

He said, 'If you really fancy yourself as a soldier, start at the bottom like anyone else.' His voice and manner changed again, and as abruptly. 'By the way, your Kolberg film is going ahead, I hear, if to a less fanciful world-outlook.'

My heart gave a leap. For all my resolutions to embrace the real world, this was different. This was the noble undertaking of which I had yearned to be a part. 'But who is making it?' I stammered. 'Who has written the screenplay?'

'Our friend Professor Harlan is writing it himself, I believe.'

As soon as I reported again to the Promi I found out all I could about the project, which was not much. A visit to the studios gathered a little more. The word was that the sky was the limit as far as the budget for the movie went. *Kolberg*, the cynics said, was already figuring prominently in the expense accounts of department heads as a key to unlock ready supplies of Reichsmarks. It was Goebbels's own love-child, and should have nothing but the best.

Heinrich George, Paul Wegener, Horst Casper and Kristina Soderbaum were all cast. Even the composer for the music was a lavish choice –

Norbert Schulte, creator of that soldier's song that had swept the world, 'Lili Marlene'. The ace Italian cinematographer Bruno Mondi was engaged behind the camera, which would of course be loaded with Agfacolor. The I.G. Farben plant was working full out to amass enough film stock. Veit Harlan, as von Damitz had said, was writing the screenplay himself. Alfred Braun was listed as co-writer, but in the scenario department they nodded their heads and guessed that if anyone was the collaborator it was the Little Doctor in the Hermann Göringstrasse.

I contrived to meet Harlan when he called at the Ministry with the first draft of his screenplay. He seemed less sleek and sure of himself than when we had last met that evening in the Reichsminister's private cinema, but Berlin in the fall of 1943 was a confusing place for everyone. In some ways it still basked in the imperial glory of 1940 or 1941; at the same time there were air-raids, breakdowns of services, the call-ups of more and more men. The war was not going well. There had been, for example, a great tank battle on the Eastfront in July of which I had heard nothing in Ireland or England, and which here in Germany the Promi had done its best to play down; apparently many hundreds of our Panzers had been lost. When they were sure they could not be overheard or reported, the disloyal discussed the possibility of defeat.

That even Veit Harlan, Reichsprofessor of the Film, was so tainted I was not to know, of course. One was only to learn years later that he was conspiring with Kristina Soderbaum for her to revert to Swedish nationality, partly to make it less easy for Goebbels to order her to play any more anti-Jew roles, partly with an eye on the future; meanwhile, needless to say, she was quite happy to be cast as the sweet young German heroine of *Kolberg*!

What I did learn from Harlan as we sipped coffee – alas, no longer real bean-coffee – was that Goebbels's Pan-European ideal survived in the script in a minor way, but the priority was once more to encourage and glorify the resistance of the ordinary German people as opposed to the colonels and the generals in their elaborate uniforms.

'The colonels and the generals will nevertheless be expected to lend their regiments and their divisions for the filming,' he added with a touch of his man-of-the-world humour.

'*Divisions?*' I asked unbelievingly, for a division comprised many thousands of troops.

'So the Reichsminister assures me. As many as are needed. It is to be what he terms a "colossal fresco".'

'Ah, yes.' I felt the pangs of jealousy a man must feel when he hears news of his former sweetheart from the man who has won her. 'Tell me, are there still the two marshals of France, one ruthless, one humane?'

He shrugged. 'I guess so. Alfred is a champion of this point' – not even my idea was left to me! 'But the English are quite banished. Would you believe it, someone actually proposed that there should be a good Englishman bringing help to Kolberg!'

'Historically, that was the case.'

'But politically no longer appropriate.' The worldly smile crinkled his eyes again.

I asked him if there might be an opportunity for me to work on the film, in any capacity. When he said he would bear me in mind with that easiness which means that, on the contrary, I would be immediately forgotten, I was scarcely aggrieved. It was not now the film of which I had dreamed. When papers arrived ordering me to report for military service I did not take them to the department chief for a deferment, as was the usual practice. If I were to be faithful to the feelings which had seized me as I returned to the Fatherland, I told myself, I should accept the call to arms.

On the first day of December, with the Berlin stores already decorated for Christmas and the old stormtroopers rattling their collecting tins for *Winterhilfe*, I exchanged the filmworld for the drills and discipline of a recruit to the infantry. On that same day I chipped off the last speck of the last reef of the Antilles on my finger nail.

After basic and specialized training I was sent with a draft of reinforcements to the Eastfront. We were assigned to a regiment in the northern sector. After the fierce battles to lift the siege of Leningrad in January, the front here was relatively quiet. We were dug in west of the River Narva which separated ancient Russia from what had been the independent state of Estonia. I had my baptism of fire but the bitter cold of winter was the grimmer enemy. I remembered the exhortations to civilians in the first winter of the Russian campaign to give up their fur coats for the troops, and the photographs we organized at the Promi of film stars smiling as they handed over their second- or third-best squirrel. Few signs of such garments remained now; certainly there was nothing left for 'fresh meat' only just arriving on the scene.

With the thaw, everyone knew, we could expect a massive Soviet offensive. The old campaigners in our company took pleasure in assuring us newcomers that we had seen nothing yet. In the event, the Russians seemed unable to break out of the bridgehead they had established across the river and capture the city of Narva. As summer came we were still in the same positions.

By now rumours of every kind swept through the troops daily. We would be transferred to the central sector, where the enemy was attacking with greater success. That was not to be relished. Or once the English and Americans made their invasion attempt, as was expected hourly, we would be sped to the West. That was much to be preferred. Most startling of all was the rumour that Germany was about to negotiate a settlement with Stalin and divert all her strength to conquering her true enemies, Churchill and Roosevelt. Where this came from remains a mystery, but the curious fact one was to learn later was that this very proposal had been made in April by none other than Josef Goebbels. He had become convinced by the public utterances of the warmongers that his previous dream of a rapprochement with the West was impossible, so had characteristically turned the billboard round to offer the opposite solution.

Finally the rumour that we were being withdrawn from the line became quite undeniable. Quartermasters were busy drawing up lists of equipment to be handed over to other units, and packing up items to be taken. As we boarded the train at the railhead, news spread like wildfire that the Anglo-Americans had landed in France. So it was to the West we were going!

With every kilometre of slow, clanking progress my comrades grew more cheerful. From somewhere some bottles of schnapps had been obtained, and soon the box-car was full of tobacco smoke and loud talk and soldiers' songs. Old Hädrich and Shithead Koppenhöfer bragged about the girls they had had in Paris or Dieppe, and laid grandiose plans to see them again. Even our sergeant, never known to smile, said that at least we should now have our arses blown off by human beings, and not the sub-humans who were the Russians.

'What about the American Negroes?' said someone.

'Propaganda,' said the sergeant.

But I have seen them! I almost blurted out. I bit back the words. I kept my previous existence to myself. And more and more it was as if I had dreamed that particular adventure. Only a year ago since I rode in the charge at Agincourt? It could more plausibly have been five hundred years and the real battle.

We were thirty hours cooped up in that damned train, held up by long waits in sidings and the usual stories of Lithuanian or Polish partisans cutting lines and attacking transports. When we were at last on German soil, and allowed to climb down and stretch our legs and empty the latrine buckets, it was night and a cool breeze brought the smell of the sea. Someone said that we were not far from Danzig. Danzig! That was not on any route to the West. Perhaps we were to regroup and exercise here before taking on a change of enemy. But a stranger rumour was already being flashed from company to company: *we were to take part in a film!*

The others received this with incredulity, I with a sinking heart. There was only one film it could be. Danzig was on the Baltic, and only 100 or 120 kilometres along the same coast lay the fortress town of Kolberg. To be carried by the blind chance of war back to the world I had fled was too cruel. Some years ago in the United States we had the English series *Brideshead Revisited* on Public Broadcast, which I watched for the appearance – one of the better ones of his old age – of Olivier. Believe me, I sympathized with the narrator of the story when he finds himself in this same position, if soon losing patience with his insipid postures thereafter.

The train clanked on, and eventually by a round-about route we came to Kolberg. Or rather, the train halted outside Kolberg for us to march directly to our camp. I went into the town when we had time off, of course; it had been much rebuilt and could not be used for filming street scenes; these were shot in a reconstruction of old Kolberg built in another location. What was it all costing? Meanwhile my comrades swore in astonishment at their first sight of what awaited us.

In one direction lines of tents stretched away as far as the eye could see. In another quarter it was as if the clock had been turned back to the Thirty

Years War. Covered wagons were clustered in ragged circles. Smoke rose from a thousand tin chimneys. Washing hung on lines, children played, dogs barked. And as we were settling into our lines we saw the menfolk returning from exercise. They rode by in drab dun uniforms, troop after troop, squadron after squadron, singing some barbaric song. They were the famous Cossacks of the Soviet general Vlassov who had deserted to our side.

Our field kitchens prepared meals as we had not tasted for months: fish from the sea, young herring, pork and good sausage, all with potatoes. In the evening the canteen sold beer. There were girls from the town or, for those acclimatized to Slavonic ideals of womanhood, from the Cossack encampment. By day we marched and formed squares according to the drills of the era. Far too few uniforms of the Grand Army had arrived to clothe the swelling muster of soldiery, so on the second day we also spent many hours plunging familiar field-grey tunics, brand-new from the stores, into tubs of dark-blue dye. Our hands and forearms were stained for days afterwards. To fake the pipe-clayed bandoliers that crossed the soldiers' breasts we were instructed to use white lavatory paper. 'At last,' said our sergeant, inspecting us, 'you wear the insignia of the shithouse grenadiers you are.'

He was a character, that sergeant. When four thousand navy men on some kind of training in Kolberg were press-ganged into the film army, he observed kindly that at least it would give them a taste of war. How many men Veit Harlan finally commanded as shooting began is anyone's guess.

They say it was more than Napoleon's marshals had for the real attack on Kolberg. Certainly there were six thousand horsemen, compared with Olivier's two hundred. If you see *Kolberg* you will see vaster armies that in any of the legendary epics.

Veit Harlan: I saw him in the distance only; his instructions were relayed by assistant directors and busybody lieutenants playing at being assistant directors. That was fine by me. I was torn, inevitably, between jealousy for the film I had helped scheme and wanting only to be a soldier like my fellow-soldiers, who took it with a shrug as an inexplicable respite from the Front.

Kristina I also saw when she came to watch the charge of the French cavalry through the sand-dunes to the west of the town. Though not to rank with the charge of the French noblemen in *Henry V*, this is a great piece of film-making. She was wearing a dirndl with a peasant blouse and her golden hair piled up, like anyone's girl back home, if prettier, and all the *Soldaten* whistled and waved. I did the same.

There is another fine piece of cinema as infantry advance in separate geometric phalanxes. I am in the second square of troops on the right flank as they approach the camera.

Finally came the 'chariot race', as Hollywood terms the climactic action sequence any action movie should build towards. For this Harlan was going to spill the waters of the River Persante to flood the town and engulf the attackers, just as Nettelbeck had done in 1808.

What a day of waiting and getting wet and trying

to follow orders that was! Six cameras were deployed, one in a captive balloon. When it was all done, there was a slug of *Korn* for everyone and Heinrich George dropped in on our company. It was a propaganda exercise, of course, but I could not help warming to the Old Commie. He told us he had trodden the stage for the first time here in the theatre in Kolberg, when he was eighteen, and the town would always be especially beloved in his eyes. It came to me that in this hundred-kilogramme heavyweight we had a kind of hero for the last days.

The radio and the soldier newspaper were now full of the retaliation or 'V-bombs' devastating England, but the war showed no signs of ceasing. Next day we returned to it. For those of us on the Eastfront it was a shorter journey than when we had come.

Fourteen

In December 1944, one year after I went into the *Wehrmacht*, my commanding officer received sudden orders for me to be sent back to Berlin. Even in the last months of the war with enemies pressing on all sides, army routine clanked on. Men were dispatched on training courses and so forth. But this was exceptional. I was to report at once to the 'cloak and dagger' establishment at Friedenthal. Fortunately, perhaps, the troop train on which I was travelling was derailed by partisans and I suffered a minor injury. By the time I reached Friedenthal the special group I should have joined had long since set off.

If you know your WWII chronology you will have guessed what that group was. The buccaneer Skorzeny had formed a commando of English-speaking troops to be dressed in American uniforms and given American equipment. Their task was to roam behind the American lines and create havoc during our last great offensive in the West, in the Ardennes. Von Damitz had perhaps remembered my existence and applied for me. He himself went as second-in-command, though his own English was stilted and academic.

For a few days excitement and hope gripped Berlin as the offensive went well. Thousands of Americans were captured; their morale was reported to be low. Goebbels talked of driving the enemy out of Europe. Then the weather improved. The enemy rallied. Our advance was halted, our petrol stocks had been squandered in vain; the war continued.

Had I been in time to take part in the operation, maybe I would be a dead man by now. Who knows? As it was, I kicked my heels at Friedenthal. Naturally, I went into poor battered Berlin whenever I could get a pass. Veit Harlan's last film before *Kolberg*, *Opfergang*, had been released after being held up by Goebbels for more than a year. I did not bother to seek it out, but I did drop in on old acquaintances at the Promi and the studios. *Kolberg* itself, I learned, had been completed only to run up against the Reichsminister in its turn. Harlan had been summoned to see him on Christmas Day, of all days, to 'discuss' further cuts. Apparently the battle scenes were considered far too bloody; they would terrify rather than inspire the people. The cutting rooms at Neubabelsberg were working deep into the night.

In mid-January the Russians launched their winter offensive and were soon deep into Poland. Part of me fretted to be back with my comrades, the more prudent part knew that nothing could stem the tide against us now. Death in action against this enemy would be one thing. To be taken prisoner and held perhaps for eternity in some barbarous camp was another matter.

The heroes of the Ardennes subterfuge returned to Friedenthal. After some days von Damitz sent for me. He had a cinema projector set up in his office, together with a screen. He said nothing while an orderly fussed with this equipment. Finally the picture flickered on to the screen, a bright greensward hemmed by knights and soldiers and, circling each other in the centre, the English King and the Constable of France.

I watched with a curious detachment as the King was hit and reeled away. Now it was my turn to be disarmed . . . then I sent his sword spinning with a blow from the mace. He lurched over below me. I strained against the stirrups, the mace raised high –

'Enough!' cried von Damitz.

The picture froze, then the screen went blank.

'I could still have you shot for that,' he said quietly. 'What happened? Was it that goddamned filmworld loyalty we hear so much of? The make-believe more important than the real?'

'I wondered if that was the explanation,' I said. 'But I don't think it is.'

'What does it matter any more?' he answered. Two small spots of colour glowed in his pale cheeks. 'Did you know that we sent word calling off the operation?'

'The Irish said something of it.'

'It was on the orders of the Führer himself. He had been told that the English victory in the film was over the French, and immediately realized that the harm to relations with the troublesome de Gaulle could only help our cause.'

I nodded.

234

'It was so simple in the Ardennes,' he said, nostalgically. 'We only had to frighten and confuse the enemy.'

Towards the end of the month I was ordered to report next morning at the Propaganda Ministry. Again I wondered, half resentfully, half in hope, if I were to end the war behind a desk. To my surprise I was ushered almost immediately into the office of Dr Naumann, Goebbels's political chief at the ministry. He asked me one or two questions whose connection I could not at first see – about my apprenticeship at the film studios, my experiences at the front, my training at Friedenthal. 'You have made a parachute descent?' was, for example, one of his questions.

'Naturally, Herr Ministerialdirigent,' I replied, though in truth it was only the descent from the tower nearly two years earlier which had given me a badly sprained ankle.

He told me that the Reichsminister wished to see me in person, if he could find the time, and I was to wait in the ante-room. I waited there all day. Finally, at about five o'clock, I was summoned.

Goebbels had aged in the year and a half since I last saw him. Though still tanned, his face showed the strain of the many different duties he had taken on. Apart from his ministry and all its ramifications, he governed the city of Berlin, directed the mobilization of the entire nation, busied himself more and more with military affairs, made practically all the speeches and radio broadcasts that were still made and continued to write his monthly article in *Das Reich*.

I am sure he had no recollection of me. Even senior members of his staff were as typewriters or duplicating machines in his office, forgotten as soon as replaced, and I had been but a very insignificant aide.

But he put on a pretence of recognition.

'Ah, Sergeant Harris,' he said – for I had won promotion at the front – 'not the most beloved of names!'

'Unfortunately not, Herr Reichsminister.' Official propaganda against the air-raids reducing our cities to ruins had lately begun to name the English air marshal Harris as the arch-villain.

'The airman Harris will yet stand in the dock as a war criminal and murderer. Victory is still within our grasp. Meanwhile, you have been chosen to perform a very special mission. Have you heard about a colour film called *Kolberg* which has just been completed?'

'Indeed, Herr Reichsminister. I had the privilege to be associated with the scenario at an early stage. As the Reichsminister will recall, it was my suggestion that the rivalry between the two French marshals should be developed – '

'It is an epic colour film,' said Goebbels, cutting me off. 'In a thousand years it will still be projected, and the citizens of the future will marvel at the spirit of a people who could make such a film at their darkest hour. They will say that the darkest hour was in fact our finest hour. As for our citizens and soldiers of today, it is a film to inspire every one to the final defence of the homeland and the victorious peace that will follow!'

It was not Goebbels's habit to waste his rhetoric on audiences of one sergeant. Three sergeants, perhaps; one, no. I guessed that he was working up a speech to be delivered in the near future. *Kolberg* was presumably about to be released. His next words confirmed this deduction.

'The Führer has personally directed that the colour film shall receive its première on the thirtieth of January, the anniversary of his coming to power twelve years ago. That is next Tuesday. He has further directed that this première shall be before an audience which best represents the indomitable spirit of the citizens of Kolberg in holding out against encircling forces.'

What could he have in mind? There were Germans surrounded at Memel, at Bromberg, maybe even at Pozen by now. According to mysterious messages reaching Friedenthal, there was even an army formation left far to the rear in the forests of Lithuania. But it was to be none of these.

Goebbels said, 'The choice has fallen on the Atlantic fortress of La Rochelle.'

La Rochelle! It was one of a number of French ports whose garrisons had been ordered to hold out to the last man when the English and Americans landed in France, so that they might not be used for shipping in supplies to the invasion forces. In the event, Montgomery had brought his own harbour with him, as my stolen plans would have warned had they been heeded. Some of the Channel ports were stormed; one surrendered with scarcely a shot fired; Lorient and St Nazaire and La Rochelle were simply sealed off and passed by. They were now a thousand kilometres from any fighting and, and as far as one knew, left to their own devices.

'The commandant of the garrison has sent a wireless message to express his appreciation of the gesture,' Goebbels was continuing. 'He says there is an excellent cinema in the town. Supplies of all sorts have been dropped from the air for six months now, with a high rate of successful recovery. In this case, however, extra precautions are necessary. It would be an eternal disgrace if our masterpiece were to fall into enemy hands before it is seen by Germans. You will parachute in with the cans of film. You will also carry grenades. Should winds carry you beyond the perimeter of our enclave, or anything happen to the aircraft on the way, you will at once destroy the film without consideration of your own person. Is that understood?'

'Perfectly, Herr Reichsminister.'

'Good. I have made arrangements for you to set off at once, in case bad weather should intervene. I am told that conditions are favourable at present. The greetings of the Führer and the German people go with you. Heil Hitler!'

The projectionist in the Defence Zone Theatre, otherwise La Rochelle's former principal fleapit, seemed perfectly competent. He was an old soldier in the signal corps and within five minutes had the newsreel I had also brought laced up in one machine, the first reel of *Kolberg* in the other. The fluctuating power of the garrison electricity supply could be a problem, he said, but tonight the commandant had promised there would be no cuts. As soon as the newsreel was running – it was a month-old edition with Christmas scenes – I guessed it safe to leave the projection box and find my way into the rear of the auditorium.

If all continued well, I planned to hobble away altogether. Bad weather and Luftwaffe indifference had conspired to make sure that I did not fly until the last chance. Then, the journey had not been exactly a joy ride: the long cold flight by Heinkel across the width of France, the terrifying moment of leaping into the murky void below with the canvas satchel containing the cans of film and grenades strapped across my chest, the heavy landing that drove the breath from my body and left me black and blue . . .

I wanted more than anything in the world to soak in a hot bath, eat, drink and sleep. In beleaguered La Rochelle these were all luxuries. The enemy, especially the French forces, kept up a constant, wearing activity of patrols and raids. Everyone was tired and jumpy. But there had been an old hotel near the submarine pens when I passed through the port on my way to Ireland, more or less the property of the boat crews. It was still open, I learned. Even a few whores continued to ply their trade there, so indelibly branded as collaborationists that they had nothing more to lose.

I had wondered what the commandant would make of my mission. There must have been many consignments he might have preferred to a patriotic movie, but he revealed nothing but soldierly correctness. The attitude expected of him was respectful gratitude to the Führer, and that is what he would

239

display. Among the troops, of course, a more sardonic reaction prevailed.

I slipped now into an empty aisle seat by the side of a pioneer corporal. Perhaps he did not see my sergeant's stars. Perhaps he did not care. He continued to mutter to the world in general that sausage or schnapps would have made more sense. I did not know what to think. From the perspective of this strange outpost it was impossible not to see that the end of the war was not far off. The only heroic course would be to die in the final battle, the Armageddon. But here in La Rochelle, even the vengeful French troops showed no great appetite for Armageddon.

The lights dimmed again. The spell of the cinema under which we had all grown up stilled the rumble of voices and the coarse laughs, at least for the moment. Now it was up to Harlan to hold the spell. I would give him ten minutes to show whether he could before slipping out.

Forty years, four thousand subsequent movies, forty thousand hours of rubbish on television have crowded out from my mind all but a few sequences of that film that night. Those that do survive play as sharply as ever if I close my eyes. The opening sequence is one of them, a marvellous bustle of troops marching and crowds surging through the streets of an ancient city. 'A storm is rising,' declared the soldier Gneisenau, played by Horst Caspar, an actor with a small trace of the heroic magnetism Goebbels so desired. A subtitle identified time and place as 'Breslau, 1813'. So we were starting with events six or seven years after the

240

beginning of the scenario as I had known it. Why was that? Ah, of course! Gneisenau was exhorting the King to rise with his subjects against Napoleon and drive him from their land. The inspiration, which he had witnessed himself, was the indomitable stand of the citizens of Kolberg when the French first arrived.

It was the conversion of a defeat into a future victory to which we had always intended to work, but now brought forward so that the story of Kolberg itself would become an enormous flashback. It was the same damned device as that of the *Lady Hamilton* film I had watched with Goebbels and Harlan and Kristina so long ago, and I still did not care for it. But it had to be admitted that it solved all the problems which von Damitz had foreseen of having a movie about the destruction and eventual fall of a town and still being able to draw positive propaganda from it. Only six years later the sacrifice is seen to be triumphantly worth while.

How would our sacrifice today be viewed today after such a short span? Six years would bring us to 1951. Who in the Devil's name could possibly imagine 1951? But suddenly, at that moment, I thought for the first time that there could be a future. This bizarre mission had finally and irreversibly set me into the lap of the West. Unless I were very unlucky or the fortress commandant proved to be a fanatic, I would become a prisoner of the Americans. The New World beckoned. Hollywood, here I come!

On the screen Napoleon had paid his respects to my illustrious namesake, and now we were in

Kolberg on New Year's Eve. They were drinking a toast to the year 1807, not knowing what it was to bring. I felt I should at least evaluate the screenplay and the performances for a few minutes more. I groped in my pocket for a packet of those powdery fruit pastilles that came in soldier rations, and offered one to the pioneer corporal before taking one myself.

Heinrich George was Nettelbeck, the burgomaster whose determination to defend his home-town shamed and antagonized the defeatist garrison commander, Colonel Loucadou, played by Paul Wegener. Historically, of course, Loucadou was not quite like that; nor was Nettelbeck the burly figure with cropped grey hair and big grey moustache that Heinrich made him. He was a slight man, the records indicated. But after seeing this characterization, you would never see Nettelbeck other than as a burly figure with cropped grey hair and big grey moustache. What a giant actor Heinrich was when it came to playing outsize characters, good or bad! He could have created the finest Churchill in cinema history.

Now Kristina had a scene. She was Nettelbeck's niece Maria, in peasant blouse with a spotted red and white kerchief at the neck, her blonde hair combed high.

The family lived outside the walls of the town in one of those beautiful Pomeranian farm-houses with a huge, steep roof. Her brother was a violinist who despised war. I could guess that both these circumstances would play their part, but didn't propose to wait to see how.

Ah, Gneisenau had replaced Loucadou and Net-telbeck was out of the town gaol and busy organizing defences. He ordered the farmers outside the town to destroy their homes rather than let them be used by the enemy. Maria's father set his on fire with his own hands. Now Nettelbeck was sending Maria by boat to Königsberg with a letter for the King of Prussia. She managed to gain an introduction to the Queen, who promised to pass the letter on and embraced its bearer. 'There are few jewels left in our crown,' she said. 'Kolberg is the most precious of them.' From somewhere angel voices sang. It was too absurd. I gathered my weary bones together to make a move. From beside me came a snort. Evidently it was too much for the pioneer corporal. I glanced at him.

It was not a snort. It was a sob.

Dear God. I had to see what happened next. Besides, the air-raid alarms were sounding.

Maria returned to a burning Kolberg. The French infantry advanced in their great square formations, myself among them. I crammed another sweet into my mouth, then another.

I surrendered. I surrendered to Nettelbeck's plan to flood the approaches to the town; to the pacifist brother trying to rescue his violin from the swirling waters and dying; to Veit Harlan's cavalry charging through the dunes; even to a little quarrel between the two French commanders, forgetting – I swear – that this was the last vestige of my other contribution to the movie.

I ignored, like everyone else, the sudden racket of the 88-mm flak battery outside the cinema. I watched Nettelbeck watch the destruction of his house in the bombardment on the screen. When the camera pulled back to take in all the town, it could have been a quarter of Hamburg after the fire storm of 1943, or a quarter of Berlin or Hanover this very day.

Except that this was make-believe and they were real. Was von Damitz right and this the explanation of my conduct – better the ruins of the set designer than the ruins of reality, better the fake blood of the make-up girl than the spilled blood of real civilians and soldiers?

No. It was something other than that as I watched old Heini and remembered Olivier. It was the certainty that we must all have heroes, for without heroes there is no hope. So who would choose to slay the King; who would dare to shoot the hero, on whosoever side he be?

I wanted this movie to go on and on for ever. While it lasted, no harm could come to us. Nettelbeck put his arms round Maria and told her such nonsense about bravery and victory, while in the shattered cathedral the people sang a hymn of thanksgiving.

In the darkness I wept for those poor heroes on the screen. I wept for all the people of my own time whose houses burned. I wept for my poor mother and my despised father, and prayed for their souls. I wept for Martin Kilner whose father, I knew, but could not tell him, had hanged himself after Martin's mother had been taken to a concentration camp. I wept for Jacko, whom I had shamefully slain with a filmworld prop. I wept for the comrades

I had left on the Eastfront. I wept for my drowned, bare Angeline. And most of all I wept for Germany.

Fifteen

I made it to America, eventually, but not as a war prisoner. Can you believe it, the idiot commandant of La Rochelle held out until 9 May, five days after the surrender of the rest of the troops in the West. Maybe *Kolberg* really inspired him. By the time the Americans had us sorted out, they needed all their ships to send their own men back across the Atlantic.

The lousy French worked me on a farm the rest of that year. Back in the ruins of Germany in 1946 I found a job first an an interpreter to the British, then with the Ford Motor Company in Düsseldorf. Five years of assiduous yes-sirring and string-pulling finally got me to the States. But it was 1952 before I found a toehold in Hollywood.

So I missed the golden years of opportunity. The first chill breezes were blowing across the studio lots as television expanded. Oh, I worked on half a dozen movies, of which the best was *The Iron Lake*, if you saw that. There was a project of my own taken up four times and likewise cancelled four times. When Lee Maxwell landed the screenplay of

Wanderlust and asked me if I could take over his classes at the Film School, I saw no reason not to give it a whirl, just for one semester.

The semester became the rest of the year, the year was followed by another, a permanency was offered. What the hell? I discovered a knack for teaching, or at least for teaching the few bright ones among the knuckleheads. Jack Behrens, Darius Pago and William Steward were all my students. Nowadays I only give my two academic courses, no more nursemaiding the kids through their dull, derivative or insane student films. If not what I dreamed of, it has been as honourable a living as most.

Married? Three times, about average for Southern California. The third, Kristi, is nearly forty years my junior and sweet, even if she needs a lot of therapy. I have daughters aged thirty-eight, thirty-six and three.

Martin Kilner called me in 1965, I think it was. He was on a trip to the States as rather a senior figure in one of the English television networks. He'd moved into TV, he told me, when magazines started to close. We met at the Scandia, talked a lot about our days at Ufa, not so much about Ireland and Olivier. It was almost as if he were too embarrassed to raise the matter of his kidnap, so in the end I bulldozed in. Said it was a necessary act of war but I was relieved he'd come to no harm, etcetera.

This out of the way, he relaxed a lot. A few weeks after he chased back to England, he said, he'd enlisted in the British Army. In some camp cinema in Palestine, at about the end of 1944, he had seen *Henry V*. The troops around him had not been

247

enthusiastic. The film had, in any case, been finished too late to fulfil its aim of inspiring the civilian population if their armies ran into bad times invading Europe. So what, I told him. It may have missed the boat to the Normandy beaches but it caught that mysterious tide that swirls just a handful of movies on to the beaches of Heaven.

Kolberg missed every damned tide. The day after our bizarre world première in La Rochelle it opened at the last two Ufa show-places left standing in Berlin, on the Alexanderplatz and the Tauentzie-strasse. But the air-raids had left the populace with little stomach for movie-going. Copies were also sent to front-line outposts in the East, to no greater effect. The supreme irony came when Kolberg itself, besieged in 1945 as it had been in 1807, surrendered to the Soviets without firing a shot.

Goebbels nevertheless remained devoted to the film. His personal secretary Rudi Semmler recorded in his diary how on 17 April 1945, just two weeks before Goebbels killed his family and himself in the bunker, he was still full of *Kolberg*. At his daily conference he seized on its example as the induce-ment with which to try and inspire the assembled lackeys and pressmen to final resistance. In a hun-dred years' time, he told them, another fine colour film would be playing. It would show the terrible days that they were all living through. 'Every one of you has the chance to choose the part you will play in that film,' he cried. 'For the sake of that prospect, it is worth standing fast. Hold out now, so that the audience a hundred years hence does not hoot and whistle when you appear on the screen.' According to Semmler this went down with the audience there and then about as well as a dose of laxative.

Veit Harlan had a hard time after the war. Because he'd directed *Jud Süss* they made him the scapegoat for all the anti-Jew films of the era; in the end he was cleared and worked again, until he died. Kristina became a photographer in Munich, Stanley Kubrick told me only two or three years ago. He'd met her there.

Von Damitz disappeared in the holocaust of Berlin. I guess he perished. I couldn't imagine him as a party kraut in the DDR. Heinrich George certainly died in Russian captivity. This is turning in to a roll-call of the dead. It has to be. Who else? Krasker, Esmond Knight, and now Olivier.

There is one other to be numbered. She haunts me still. So much that for the last ten years I have been unable to go swimming. To live in California and not swim! It's unique. Sometimes Kristi wakes me at night to say she's scared, I've stopped breathing or been choking or whatever, and some of the sometimes I have the taste of old brown water in my mouth. As Kristi goes to sleep again and I lie awake, and that scene in the moonlit lake plays in my mind once again, it gets more and more like a movie. These days I'm always looking on it as a spectator. I see her, I see me.

I read that all our television emissions since television began are beaming out into space. The game shows, the newscasts, the soaps, the movies, they go speeding on for ever. And when, in many thousands of years from now, our civilization is dead and the scholars of some distant world study signals monitored from Earth, how will they ever be able to distinguish between our dreams and our history, our myths and our reality, our truth and our lies?